THE ECSTASY TREE

Indira found the girl. She found her pressed tightly against the trunk of the tree that from a distance had looked like a weeping willow. Her arms had been forced back, held by several green tendrils. Her legs had been forced open, also held by tendrils. Her fatigue dress had been torn and her full breasts exposed—tendrils gripped them. Tendrils had also ripped her trousers and entered her. And one crimson-stained tendril had wrapped itself round her neck.

Her eyes were closed, her mouth sagging open. Her breasts twitched and shuddered, but she did not seem to care, or be conscious of anything.

The green tree still had a great many "weeping" green thongs, deceptively limp but hideously powerful. Indira set the laser on maximum burn. She couldn't blast the tree itself for fear of hurting the girl; but she could and did burn the weeping tendrils.

She burned them ferociously. The green stuff hissed and crackled. Pungent black smoke rose up to the sky. . . .

Fawcett Gold Medal Books
by Richard Avery:

THE EXPENDABLES

#1   THE DEATHWORMS OF KRATOS

#2   THE RINGS OF TANTALUS

The Expendables #2

THE RINGS OF TANTALUS

by

Richard Avery

A FAWCETT GOLD MEDAL BOOK

Fawcett Publications, Inc., Greenwich, Connecticut

THE EXPENDABLES #2

THE RINGS OF TANTALUS

Copyright © 1975 by Richard Avery

Printed in the United States of America

First printing: October 1975

1 2 3 4 5 6 7 8 9 10

CONTENTS

STAGE ONE

ORBIT

		Page
Memorandum		10
Phase One	Defrost	16
Phase Two	Joker In The Pack	22
Phase Three	The Moon That Wasn't	31
Phase Four	Enigma Variation The First	41
Phase Five	Enigma Variation The Second	53
Phase Six	Israeli Logic	58

STAGE TWO

TOUCH-DOWN

Phase One	Touch-Down And Revelations	64
Phase Two	Tale Of A Prehensile Tail	69
Phase Three	The Kwango Scenario	77
Phase Four	Heads You Win, Tails You Lose	84
Phase Five	Crash!	89
Phase Six	A Call To Arms	98
Phase Seven	Enter The U.S. Cavalry	103

STAGE THREE

SHOWDOWN

Phase One	The Impatient Patient	108
Phase Two	Kwango's Tango	114
Phase Three	Conrad Gets Tough	125
Phase Four	Sudden Death	131
Phase Five	Conrad Stirs It Up	141

Phase Six	A Bad Day For Expendables	147
Phase Seven	Khelad Falls Out Of A Tree	157
Phase Eight	Go For Broke!	164
Phase Nine	Winner Takes All – The Final Scenario	175
Phase Ten	Mission Ends	186
Memorandum		191

THE RINGS OF TANTALUS

Stage One

ORBIT

MEMORANDUM

To: Secretary General, United Nations.
From: Director, Extra-Solar Planets Evaluating and Normalising Department.
Most Secret. For your eyes only.
Subject: The Proving of Tantalus, 7th planet Alpha Leonis (Regulus), distance 56 light years.
3rd March 2074 S.E.T.

Para 1. You are already aware of increasing opposition from certain Third World countries to the ExPEND programme for investigating distant planets that may be suitable for colonisation. As you know, this opposition is based on the high cost of the robot probes used for initial investigation, and the far higher cost of following up preliminary investigation by committing a suitably equipped team of Expendables, in a faster-than-light vessel, to discover if human beings can survive on such a planet.

Para 2. Despite the fact that the first project, the proving of Kratos, was brought to a successful conclusion, Third World opposition continues to intensify. You cannot fail to have noticed that the most vociferous opponents are certain South American countries (notably Brazil and Argentina), certain Arab countries (notably Algeria, Libya and Egypt) together with three or four central African states and, of course, Indonesia.

Para 3. The success of the Kratos venture (ref. File One, Appendix One, ExPEND Report, December '73) demonstrates that the future of mankind need no longer be determined by the dwindling resources of the Solar System. A thriving and expanding colony now exists on Kratos. Latest information indicates that the population of Jamestown exceeds 2,500; 220 of its people being indigenously born. We shall continue to use matter transmission until the population has reached 10,000. This, I am assured by the geneticists, will provide a sufficiently varied genetic pool for Kratos to proceed independently with its own expansion. Naturally, the emigrants will be drawn from all terrestrial nations; and, in fact, a high proportion will come from Third World countries.

Para 4. This, however, does not diminish opposition—as you are aware from the proceedings of the last session of the General Assembly. So long as such opposition is of a political and democratic nature, future ExPEND programmes are not at risk. Investigation, proving and colonisation will continue until U.N. decrees otherwise.

Para 5. But an alarming new factor has developed. I have received a report from the C.I.A. of the United States of America (later confirmed by the External Security Department of the Soviet Union) that sabotage of ExPEND is now being actively encouraged by various clandestine organisations supported by funds from one or more of the countries mentioned in Para 2.

Para 6. It has been suggested that ExPEND itself has been infiltrated by hostile elements, especially in the division concerned with the preliminary selection of suitable candidates for the proving teams. A discreet security check has already revealed that three members of the Selection Group obtained their position by assuming false identities.

We are unable to trace the people whose identities were adopted by the infiltrators. They are presumed dead.

Para 7. As these members of the Selection Group played a significant part in choosing the small group from which Commander James Conrad drew four new recruits to make up the team for Project Tantalus, it must be assumed that one or more saboteurs were included.

Para 8. I need not remind you that, because of the hazardous nature of such operations, each team of Expendables is composed of talented and/or highly qualified social misfits, outcasts and criminals. This policy was decided upon because the dangers of planet proving are unknowable. At the same time such limitations make the introduction of possible saboteurs relatively easy.

Para 9. The team assigned to the proving of Tantalus left the Solar system before I became aware of the possibility of sabotage. By now, their F.T.L. vessel, The *Santa Maria* (modified after the Kratos venture according to Commander Conrad's requirements), should be in planetary orbit. A message has been despatched to Commander Conrad apprising him of the new situation.

Para 10. Although five of the original Kratos team returned to the Solar System in good health (one was killed on Kratos, and one died later as a result of irreversible brain damage), Commander Conrad is now accompanied by only two of his former companions. By my authority, Fidel Batista and Chantana Le Gros were seconded for the training of future teams.

Para 11. For your convenience I append a list of the present complement of the *Santa Maria,* together with relevant data.

Para 12. In view of the information provided in this most secret memorandum, I humbly request that you use *all* the facilities of your high office to actively discourage opposition to and sabotage of the ExPEND programme as approved by U.N. Third World anxieties are understandable. It is true that the vast amounts of capital, technology and energy assigned for the development of extra-solar colonisation could be used to alleviate—if only temporarily —the condition of millions of starving people in Asia, Africa and South America. But the issue is not a short-term one. The ultimate issue is the survival of mankind. To ensure that, we need new worlds.

APPENDIX I

Complement of *Santa Maria* re proving of Planet Seven, Alpha Leonis.

Conrad, James. Age 39. Commander Expendables, Team Two. Nationality, British. Ex-commander United Nations Space Service, formerly captain. Distinguished Space Service Cross and bar. Resigned from U.N.S.S. after being reduced to rank of commander and forfeiting ten years' seniority as result of court-martial. Court martial findings (presided over by Admiral Kotuzov): guilty as charged in wilfully and repeatedly disobeying orders of commanding officer when permission to attempt rescue of crew of *S.S. Einstein* in decaying solar orbit was denied; not guilty of putting at risk safety of *S.S. Garagin* which he then commanded; guilty of bringing about the deaths of three of his crew members and one engineer officer in aforementioned attempted rescue. Conrad was himself badly injured—one arm severed by mooring cable, one eye burned out by solar radiation. Now has prosthetic right arm. Elected also to have infra-red eye implanted in vacant right socket, normally covered by silver patch.

After successful proving of Kratos was awarded Grand Cross of Gagarin and offered restored rank of captain in U.N.S.S. Offer declined. Elected to remain Expendable.

Smith, Indira, Age 31. Second-in-Command, Expendables, Team Two. Nationality, Indian. Ex-Surgeon Lieutenant, Terran Disaster Corps. Resigned commission as a result of torture and severe injuries by so-called guerillas in Brazil. Now has two prosthetic legs. Awarded Distinguished Space Service Cross for services rendered on Kratos.

Kwango, Kurt. Age 34. Ecologist, Expendables, Team Two. Nationality, Nigerian. Previously convicted criminal with history of violence. Behaviour since recruitment by ExPEND irreproachable. Granted free pardon for crimes rendered on Kratos.

Khelad, Ahmed. Age 27. Weapons and explosives expert, felon. Nationality, Syrian. Convicted by U.S. court for hijacking and murder at Kennedy International Airport. Volunteer Expendable. Released from prison under U.N. Mandate 31-B-9-72 and placed in custody of ExPEND for indefinite period.

Pushkin, Alexei. Age 35. Engineer, felon. Nationality, Russian. Convicted by Soviet court of murder at Leningrad. Volunteer Expendable. Released from prison under U.N. Mandate 31-B-9-72 and placed in custody of ExPEND for indefinite period.

Zonis, Ruth. Age 26. Biologist, felon. Nationality, Israeli. Convicted by Egyptian court of attempted theft at Cairo. Volunteer Expendable. Released from prison under U.N. Mandate 31-B-9-72 and placed in custody of ExPEND for indefinite period.

Uhlmann, Lisa. Age 29. Chemist, felon. Nationality, American. Convicted by Mexican court for kidnapping at

Mexico City. Volunteer Expendable. Released from prison under U.N. Mandate 31-B-9-72 and placed in custody of ExPEND for indefinite period.

APPENDIX II

Records of Conrad, Smith, Kwango justify assumption of integrity. Khelad's crime was political in nature. Pushkin's crime was of personal nature. Zonis's crime was political. Uhlmann's crime was political. All three "politicals" are high risk possibilities reference sabotage. Commander Conrad is familiar with their dossiers.

DEFROST

The message had been received by sub-space radio before Conrad came out of suspended animation. Matthew had acknowledged it, as requested. Matthew was one of six self programming robots, type S.P.9. But Matthew was something special: he was S.P.9/1. He had command circuitry that could override the circuitry of the other five robots. For convenience, the robots were called Matthew, Mark, Luke, John, Peter and Paul. Their names were painted on their chest plates and back plates. All except John and Paul had worked with Commander James Conrad on the proving of Kratos. The original John and Paul had been destroyed on Kratos—one had fallen down a deep shaft and the other had been flattened by a death worm. The replacements were identical. They even had the same memory patterns programmed into them. It was, so Conrad supposed, a kind of mechanical substitute for immortality.

Because of the immense amount of energy needed for sub-space radio communication, the signal from Earth had been necessarily brief, as also had the reply.

The message read: *Possible saboteur in your team. Take necessary steps. Vital Tantalus project succeeds. Message ends. Signal receipt. Director, ExPEND.*

The reply read: *Acknowledged S.P.9/1 p.p. Conrad.*

Conrad, still shaky from the trauma of emerging from

suspended animation, contemplated this news as he sipped coffee on the navigation deck of the *Santa Maria*, now in a stable 2,000 kilometre orbit round Tantalus.

A saboteur . . . Well, it was possible. Not probable, he thought, but possible. He had been on Terra after the Kratos mission long enough to catch up on domestic politics. He knew well enough that certain prominent people in certain countries had been very noisy about their objection to the ExPEND programme. He did not blame them. They were concerned with local problems— ever-increasing population, disease, protein shortage, the inexorable decrease of fertile land areas, the shortage of fossil fuels, famine, crime, revolution and all the ills that an over-populated planet is heir to. Yes their problems were local and immediate. They were too busy, too har-rassed, to concern themselves with the biggest problem of all—the long-term one of racial survival.

Who could blame them if they screamed at the vast amounts of money, science, energy that were siphoned off into deep space exploration? The probing of Kratos had ensured, at least, that mankind's ultimate fate need not be limited to the confines of the solar system. But what con-solation was that to people who needed to catch votes in order to govern under steadily deteriorating conditions?

Conrad glanced through the observation panel. The *Santa Maria* was passing over the sunside of Tantalus. It looked very beautiful—much as Earth looked from close orbit. The oceans were green, blue, iridescent. The three major continents were rich in vegetation. The enigmatic rings the probes had revealed were too small to be seen by the naked eye. Conrad's instincts told him that he was going to have enough problems when the *Santa Maria* touched down on the surface of that deceptively tranquil planet, without having to worry about a possible saboteur. Or saboteurs . . . Now there was a nasty thought. What if it turned out that there was more than one?

But why the devil should even the most rabid Third World politicos want to destroy a mission that was ultimately in their own interests and to which the money, energy, and know-how had already been committed? He got the answer almost immediately. It wasn't just that they might wish to wreck the Tantalus project. That would gain them nothing. It had to be a gambit by which the whole ExPEND operation would be discredited. That way, the enormous funds involved could be rechanneled to meet some of the needs of the hungry nations.

Yes, it made sense. Besides, ExPEND would not blast such a message across fifty-six light-years unless they believed there was a real threat. Conrad felt a tingle of fear on his spine. He had not been out of S.A. long, and he was still feeling weak and disoriented. As if, he thought bitterly, I don't have enough bloody problems on my hands.

At that moment, Matthew came onto the navigation deck.

"Sir, Lieutenant Smith is approaching viability. Do you wish to be present when she returns to consciousness?"

Conrad scratched his silver eye-patch, realised he was doing so, realised it was a stupid mannerism, and stopped it.

"No. Get her operational as fast as you can, that's all. Then pull Kwango out. Get him viable, also, as fast as you can. But don't pull out the rest until further orders."

"Decision noted. Execution proceeds," said Matthew imperturbably.

"And, Matthew, have one of your minions bring me

some more hot coffee. This stuff tastes like liquid crap."

"Query, sir. Please define the term liquid crap. The coffee was prepared by John according to programme specification number P-17-3904 and should be—"

"Cancel statement," snapped Conrad. "Get Smith and Kwango out fast, and send me some fresh coffee."

"Decision noted. Execution proceeds." Matthew left the navigation deck.

Conrad let out a great sigh. He was in an irritable mood and he knew it. He had been through it all before. The trauma of coming out of suspended animation was taking longer to wear off than he had anticipated. It was a pity you had to freeze people to transport them in starships by faster-than-light drive. But if you did not, the experience would make them mad. Oddly, F.T.L. didn't affect robots. They just went into low alert and waited patiently.

Conrad paced about nervously. Being a trained spaceman he had long ago become expert at walking on bondfuzz carpeting in a field of zero gravity. He wondered if he should have accepted Matthew's discreet suggestion that he should be present when Indira opened her eyes.

He had been present when she woke up in the I.C. unit when the *Santa Maria* was orbiting Kratos. He could still remember vividly the way she screamed when she saw his silver patch and, for a few moments, did not recognise his face. He remembered also the way Matthew, wearing the thermal gloves, had pinched and stroked her small, pallid breasts, expertly bringing massage and heat close to the heart. And he remembered the thin lines indicating the joining of living thighs to prosthetic legs. He didn't want to go through all that again. Matthew was expert in resuscitation techniques. Let him get on with the process.

Conrad, being an honest man, knew very well why he did not wish to be present at Lieutenant Smith's recall. He had lain between those prosthetic legs with much pleasure on Kratos and later in the North West Highlands of Scotland, when the Expendables had been granted leave after the success of the first mission.

He did not want to see a sexless robot manipulating the body of someone he had held with love and passion.

The robot John came to the navigation deck. "Coffee, sir, Sweet, black, eighty-five degrees centigrade." He presented the plastic bulb to Conrad.

Conrad took a squirt. It was better than the last half litre. In fact, it wasn't bad at all.

"You took your bloody time about it," he said grudgingly.

Query, sir," said John. "Please define the term bloody time."

Conrad's irritability escalated to anger. "You are a stupid, peripatetic conglomeration of electronic idiocy." Then he sighed once more, and pulled himself together. "Cancel both statements."

"Decision noted," said John impassively. "Execution proceeds. Statements one and two are now cancelled."

Conrad sipped his coffee and tried to condition himself to wait patiently for the emergence of Lieutenant Smith. Apart from the supposed or real threat of sabotage, there was plenty to think about. How long should he allow the *Santa Maria* to remain in orbit. Where should touch-down be? Should he try to get as near to one of the enigmatic rings as possible, or should he prudently make the first touch-down at a respectable distance? How long should he allow for surface adaptation to a field of—78G?

The moon of Tantalus drifted past the observation panel unnoticed. Presently, Conrad's head began to ache. Presently, he summoned a robot and demanded a quarter litre bulb of brandy from general stores. Presently Matthew informed him that Lieutenant Smith was alive and well.

Conrad's headache had gone. Whether it was due to the brandy or to the news brought by Matthew he did not know.

"How long will it take to get Kwango out?"

"Approximately one hundred and sixty-five minutes, Commander."

"Get him out faster."

"Query. Is the situation designated as an emergency, sir?"

"No, dammit. Don't take any risks. I need Kwango all in one piece." Then he added maliciously: "The last time you tried to raise him to room temperature, he was stone cold dead. Lieutenant Smith had to give him a heart transplant."

"I recall the incident, sir," said Matthew, with, perhaps, a hint of reproach in his robotic voice. "The vessel was orbiting Kratos. Cardiac failure was not due to any fault in resuscitation techniques."

"I know that," said Conrad. "Apparently, Kurt ducked his sub-thermol shock injection on Terra. So ice crystals formed and burst his heart when he was chilled. He learned his lesson. Just get him out as fast as you can. Execute."

"Decision noted, Commander. Execution proceeds."

Phase Two

JOKER IN THE PACK

Conrad held his conference in the saloon. Lieutenant Smith and Kurt Kwango, being very recently out of S.A., were ravenously hungry. Conrad watched them attack massive genuine Scotch steaks washed down with real red wine. Even on Earth, such a meal would have cost a very great deal. Add to that the cost of transporting such food fifty-six light-years, and the meal was worth more than its weight in platinum. Conrad had satisfied his own intense protein hunger some time ago. It was odd, he reflected, how everyone coming out of S.A. had this tremendous protein hunger. No doubt the medicos would explain it in terms of temporary alterations in body chemistry caused by the shock of being returned to normal temperature.

Well, he reflected, let them both enjoy their luxury. Soon they would be eating synthetic concentrates, recycled food, or living on whatever Tantalus would provide. Indira, he thought, was already beginning to look her usual attractive self. The white hair was a perfect frame for her delicate features and for the subtly light Indian skin. He remembered, briefly, the ten days they had spent together in the North West Highlands of Scotland, after returning from Kratos. A wonderful ten days to be locked away in some secret part of the mind and be treasured for ever. He pushed the memory back into its dark mental capsule.

Until Tantalus was proved, he did not want to take it out again. Until Tantalus was proved, he supposed, Indira would have to be Lieutenant Smith, Second-in-Command, Expendables Team Two.

Kwango seemed to be in great form. Unlike the last time, when Surgeon Lieutenant Smith had had to cut out his dead heart and implant a new one. The Nigerian ecologist had a magnificent physique, which showed little trace of the fact that his mother was German. The negro genes were dominant.

"So, Boss, we got problems," said Kwango with a broad smile. "Somebody wants to bust up de party, and we don't know who it is."

"We must not take it for granted that there is a saboteur in the cooler," said Conrad. "For all we know, the four recruits still on ice may be first class Expendables. The training programme showed that they were all outstanding."

"It would," retorted Kwango. "Anybody planted would have to prove that he—or she—was damn good . . . No, Commander. They didn't send you that message just to make you nervous. If we assume that one or more of our cool friends is going to remain cool towards us when brought up to room temperature, we may live a little longer."

"Have you had a chance to look at their files again?" asked Lieutenant Smith.

Conrad nodded. "It didn't make me any wiser. In theory, Alexei Pushkin, being Russian, should be above suspicion. He was convicted for murdering his wife. Oddly, she was a U.N. delegate. Even more oddly, at a press conference, she went on record as saying that Third World countries were already getting too much aid and

doing little to help themselves. She said that unless various
South American and Arab countries accepted a strict programme of birth control, they ought to be left to fend
for themselves. Incidentally, the motive for murder
established at Pushkin's trial was jealousy. It seems the
late Mrs. Pushkin was pretty generous with her favours—
particularly where they might help her political career."

Kwango gave a low whistle. "So Alexei, our friend and
brother, might have knocked her off not for laying but
for saying?"

Conrad gave a faint smile. "Precisely. We have a similar
difficulty with Lisa Uhlmann. Though she is American,
her particular crime consisted of holding the U.S. Am-
bassador to Mexico for ransom. She wanted the U.S.
to increase its aid to Latin-American countries by fifteen
percent. And how do you like that?"

"Not greatly, Boss." Kwango laughed. "But, as your
resident genius, I now proclaim that a pattern is going to
emerge. We are going to find reasons for suspecting all
four. Right?"

"Right."

"Wrong," said Lieutenant Smith. "Ruth Zonis is an
Israeli. I got to know her fairly well on the training programme. She is absolutely dedicated to the programme of
extra-solar colonisation. Also, she comes from a small but
highly efficient country that solved all its own problems
the hard way and now has a highly integrated and independent economy. She has no motive for aiding and
abetting Third World blackmail."

"Ruth Zonis," said Conrad drily, "is a very idealistic
woman. She was one of a team of Israelis sentenced to
twenty years hard labour by an Egyptian court for trying
to lift just about half the treasures of the Pharaohs from

Cairo Museum. The aim was a subtle one. They were not trying to gain anything directly for Israel. That would have brought about yet another Arab-Israeli conflict. They simply wanted to blackmail U.N. into giving the Arab countries the know-how and the resources for turning their deserts into fertile agricultural lands. That way, they thought, it would be possible to cool the old Arab-Israeli feud for good."

Lieutenant Smith shook her head. "I still think Lisa would not dream of sabotage. She is not stupid. She knows that the colonisation programme is set apart from any political manoeuvres on Earth. It isn't dominated by American or Russian or Third World thinking. She knows that the long-range issue is simply racial survival."

"And I bet she also knows," said Kwango drily, "that if ExPEND folded, the Arabs would get a lot more aid. Idealists are very dangerous people." He grinned. "Especially if they happen to be women."

Lieutenant Smith said nothing, merely contenting herself with gazing at Kwango coldly.

"The Number One Suspect, of course," resumed Conrad, "is Ahmed Khelad. Ironically, he was on the same kick as Zonis. Only Khelad tackled it the Arab way. He and three of his friends took over a fully laden jumbo passenger rocket at Kennedy. They threatened to lift off and come down with a bump on the U.N. building if aid to North African countries was not increased by several billion solars. Fortunately, that kind of gambit had been anticipated. Three C.I.A. agents were already aboard. There was a shoot-out, and the Arabs were chopped before they could blow the rocket. All the C.I.A. men died, and so did all the Arabs except Khelad." He gave a grim smile. "An American matron threw herself on him before he could trigger the charges."

"So," said Kwango, almost gaily, "we are left with the following range of possibilities—in descending order of absurdity. One, all four of our chilled comrades are saboteurs; two, none of our chilled comrades are saboteurs; three, one or more are saboteurs."

Conrad shrugged. "I'm afraid that is about it."

"What are you going to do?" asked Indira.

"As Kurt would say: let us consider the options. One, we keep them all in the cooler and try to prove the planet ourselves. Two, we bring them out of S.A. and proceed as if we had not a care in the world. Three, we get them up and caution them that one may be a saboteur. That forewarns the joker, of course—if there is a joker—but it also forewarns the others."

"There is a fourth option, Boss." Kwango smiled. "It may have escaped your notice because your I.Q. is somewhat less than mine."

Conrad let out a sigh. "Kurt, don't let yourself get fined one booze ration for insubordination so early in the game. Now, what is the fourth option?"

"We only take three out. We don't tell them anything; but we ensure that one of us is always working with one of them. That way, if there are any 'accidents' we will know who the naughty boy or girl is."

Indira said: "It's the best suggestion yet."

Conrad was silent for a while. "It's probably the best form of insurance that can be devised," he said. "But it won't work for long. There will be far too much to do for the three of us."

"I know that, Commander," said Kwango. "We can work out a shift system with, at certain times, one of us supervising two or maybe all three simultaneously. If there is a sabotage merchant with us, I'm betting it won't be too long before the action starts. Also, the stress factor may become apparent before he or she presses the button." A thought seemed to strike him. "I suppose it has to be a kami-haze job?"

Conrad nodded. "I think so. If one survivor managed to get back to Terra in the *Santa Maria*, he'd get the polygraph treatment, truth drugs—the lot. And then the whole thing would be blown."

Kwango brightened. "Good. That makes it easier. Someone who knows he is under sentence of death has to be pretty damn good not to lose his cool."

"What about us?" asked Indira. "The stress factor may cause one of us to crack too."

Kwango shrugged. "It may," he conceded. "But this is not our first mission. We have had it rough before and we haven't cracked. Also, we only *think* we may get smashed. If there is a saboteur, he *knows* he is heading for de big dark. There's a difference."

Conrad said: "Supposing I do accept your suggestion, Kurt. There's still the problem of who we leave in the cooler, and how we explain this decision to the others."

Kwango laughed. "No problem, Massa Boss."

"Cut the Uncle Tom stuff," said Conrad gently, "or I'll pound your hard black head into a jelly."

"Kindly note, Lieutenant," said Kwango, "dat de good Commander shows signs of being de fust to crack. Mebbe he is de bad man we bin lookin' for."

Conrad raised his prosthetic arm menacingly.

"Sorry, Boss," said Kwango hastily. "My sense of humour runs away with me at times . . . The choice obviously lies between Pushkin and Khelad. Logically, we have to bring out Zonis and Uhlmann."

"Why?" enquired Lieutenant Smith.

"Because women are more vulnerable than men," said Kwango with a hint of malice. "Saving your presence, Lieutenant, this is something I know from personal experience."

Conrad gave a faint smile. "He's right, of course . . . Women are more vulnerable." He gave Indira a sly glance. "But that does not necessarily make them any easier to deal with. Still, if either Zonis or Uhlmann is the bad apple, we should stand a reasonable chance of finding out before it is too late."

"Don't underestimate women," retorted Lieutenant Smith. "The female can be more deadly than the male. There's still the problem of who we leave in S.A. And there is the additional problem of how we explain it to the rest."

Kwango gave a big smile. "No problem about the explanation, Lieutenant. The heart is all bust up—like mine was when we went to Kratos. You gave me a new heart while we were in orbit. But they don't know that. You can say you can't operate in zero G."

"Agreed," said Conrad. "At least it buys us some time. I have my own ideas about who should remain chilled, but I would like to have both your recommendations."

"Khelad," said Kwango.

"Pushkin," said Lieutenant Smith.

"Why? You first, Lieutenant."

"Because I don't believe Pushkin is the kind of man to commit what the French call *crime passionel* . . . I like him. His record shows that he is a brilliant engineer. Also he is an International Grand Master of chess. I do not think he would kill because of sexual jealousy. *If* we have a saboteur, Alexei Pushkin is a strong candidate. He is the kind of man who would not destroy for personal motives but only for ideas."

"Well, Kwango?"

"I go along with much of what Lieutenant Smith says. Alexei is a nice guy, but very cerebral . . . Boss, I declare my prejudices. I don't like Arabs. They were the first slavers. They sold my people into slavery long before the first white man cut himself in on the percentage. They are real tough when the odds are with them; but when the odds are against them, they melt into the night. History shows they have a weakness for dark alleys and knives. Tantalus is a dark alley, and I am betting that Khelad has a sharp knife."

"That's settled, then," said Conrad. "We keep Pushkin chilled."

Kwango was amazed. "Why, Commander?"

"Because if Khelad is the one, the sooner we find out, the better our chances of survival. I will delay touch-down for a while, on some pretext or other. He would doubtless have many excellent opportunities once we begin the proving programme. But while the *Santa Maria* remains in orbit, his opportunities will be more limited. Naturally, I shall do my best to limit the access of all our new comrades to sensitive areas of the vessel. The robots can help. I will have one on permanent duty in the engine-room and other sensitive areas. They will be instructed not to allow anyone to pass unless accompanied by one of us."

At that moment, Matthew came into the saloon.

"Permission to report, sir?"

"Permission granted."

"Luke has remained on observation duty on the navigation deck, as you required, Commander. He reports that there are two bright objects, provisionally classified as satellites or moons, orbiting the planet Tantalus."

"So what?" snapped Conrad irritably. "Luke is a bloody—" Then the implication hit him.

"Query, sir. What bloody object—presumed—is Luke?"

"Cancel statement. What data has Luke acquired?"

"Satellite one, designated as moon of Tantalus, conforms to mass, orbit and velocity as reported by robot probe. Identification positive. Satellite two was not reported by robot probe. Mass estimated at one point five million tonnes, Earth norm at G one. Orbit eccentric. Present distance from *Santa Maria*'s orbit two hundred and forty thousand kilometres approximately, Relative velocity three thousand one hundred kilometres per hour, approaching."

Conrad stood up. "Let's get to the navigation deck on the double."

Lieutenant Smith was puzzled. "What's it all about?"

"Tantalus has only one moon, Lieutenant," said Kwango. Then he added reproachfully. "You should know that."

"This other thing," said Conrad, "is either a damned small asteroid or a damned big space ship. Come on, move!"

Phase Three

THE MOON THAT WASN'T

By the time they reached the navigation deck, Luke and the *Santa Maria*'s sophisticated system of telemetry had provided more interesting data about the "moon" that theoretically should not exist. It was metallic, it was completely symmetrical, it was ovoid, it was two point two-five kilometres long, and was point nine-five kilometres wide at its widest point.

Conrad gazed at it through the manual telescope in awe. Because it was still bathed in the bright sunlight of Regulus, he could not pick out any detail, even at seventy-five magnifications. But experience and intuition told him what the object was beyond any shadow of doubt. Kwango and Lieutenant Smith peered through the observation panel. All they could see was a bright, tiny egg.

Conrad stepped back from the telescope. When he spoke, his voice was shaking. "We are privileged—if that is the right word—to be present at the high point of human history." He gestured to the telescope. "Take a look, Kurt, and tell me what you see."

Kwango adjusted the telescope and gazed intently. "I see a bloody big cosmic egg, Commander."

"Now you, Indira."

Lieutenant Smith made a further adjustment to the eyepiece. "The same," she reported. "I see the same as Kurt, James. What is it?"

Irrelevantly, Conrad remembered another time she had called him James. It had been in a small cottage in the North West Highlands of Scotland. They were in bed together, naked, and at the point of mutual ecstasy. He thrust the memory away. That was in another country on the other side of the sky. And, besides, the wench was now Lieutenant Smith, Expendable.

"It is the proof that man is not the only clever animal to raise his covetous eyes to the stars, Lieutenant. That object is an alien space vessel. It is to the *Santa Maria* as the *Queen Elizabeth* was to the *Golden Hind*." He let out a great sigh. "I very much fear we are about to meet our masters."

"If we are about to meet our masters, Commander," said Kwango, "why the devil haven't those big boys sent out any signals? If they are all that hot, they have got to have steam radio, for starters. They must be aware of our presence. Why no noise on the old squawk box?"

Conrad shrugged. "I don't know, Kurt." He turned to the robot Luke. "Sweep all radio frequencies for signals. Execute."

"Decision noted, Commander. Execution proceeds."

"Matthew, signal on all frequencies—use variable pitch signals. We must assume that their audible range may be vastly different from ours. Make the signals simple. Transmit the numerals one to ten. Let a one-second pulse equal one, two one-second pulses equal two, and so on. Repeat the transmissions for one hour S.E.T. or until contact is established. If contact is established, let me know immediately. Execute."

"Decision noted, Commander. Execution proceeds." Matthew, imperturbable as always, joined Luke at the communications console.

"What are you going to do, James?" Indira shivered. "As if we didn't already have enough problems."

"Lieutenant Smith," said Conrad coldly, "as of now we are at action stations. It may be—and I devoutly hope so —that the alien vessel has no aggressive intentions. But we cannot know, and must make no assumptions. I need hardly remind you that the *Santa Maria* has no defensive armament. So, unless we can establish contact and somehow define our own peaceful intentions, we risk being blasted out of orbit at the best, or being totally destroyed at the worst. Such weapons as we have were designed for planetary use." He gave a grim smile. "The bright boys at ExPEND never thought we might have to take on another space-borne species. But we can adapt our weapons. We have lasers and explosives . . . Kwango, see what can be done to manufacture explosive war-heads. The robots will assist you, as required. Lieutenant Smith, see to the supercharging of three laser rifles. Also, check three space-suits and life-support systems, together with the necessary jet-packs."

Kwango said: "O.K. Commander, I hear and obey. But I think you are wasting our time."

"Why? Tell it fast, black man. I'm in no mood for the funnies."

"I think that vessel is dead. If it wasn't, they would have made noises. As you say, it's a hell of a lot bigger than we are, and it probably contains a hell of a lot of sophisticated equipment. Just begins to look like nobody's using it, that's all."

"Maybe you are right. But there is a creature on Earth that plays dead until it is sure of its prey. We can't take chances . . . Lieutenant Smith, why are you not checking out the suits as ordered?"

Indira said coldly: "Sir, I request permission to apply emergency resuscitation to our four comrades. We may need them."

"Permission denied. At a time like this, we don't want to have to worry about who is going to stab us in the back. Get moving."

"Yes, sir." She saluted insolently and left the navigation deck with Kwango.

Conrad sighed. So much for the idyll in the North West Highlands of Scotland. He turned to Matthew. "Any sign of life?"

"Query, sir. What criteria are to be applied for recognition of—"

"Cancel question," interrupted Conrad wearily. "Is there any response to transmission of signals?"

"None, Commander."

"Continue transmissions. Also programme master computer with relevant data concerning alien object's mass, velocity and orbit. Request astrogation sequence for fastest possible rendezvous of *Santa Maria* with alien object. Also request computer to develop F.T.L. Earth destination programme in case we need to get out of here fast."

"Decisions noted, Commander. Execution proceeds."

Six hours later, Conrad decided to go for broke. There had been no response of any kind from the huge alien vessel. So he decided to pay it a visit. The computer had revealed that its orbit was a vast eccentric one—which was probably why the robot probe had not registered its existence. Though of course, it was entirely possible that the vessel had entered the Regulus system after the probe's departure. Whatever the explanation, Conrad knew he could not proceed with the proving of Tantalus without attempting to resolve the mystery.

He called Kwango and Lieutenant Smith to the navigation deck.

"What's the weapons situation, Kurt?"

"Not good, but not too bad. I have had two of the robots, Mark and John, constructing a battery of six laser rifles mounted in the air-lock. All the rifles can be triggered simultaneously and the beams can be brought to focus on a given point if we know the exact range. It should be effective on carbon steel at, say, five thousand metres. Also Peter and Paul have attached spheres of cold nitro—which you may recall, was Fidel's *specialité de la maison*—on to the heads of three distress rockets. Extreme range estimated at fifteen thousand metres." Kwango shrugged. "Trouble is, Boss, we haven't had an opportunity to prove these gadgets."

"Let us hope we don't need them."

"Amen to that. I'm praying on it and I'm betting on it."

"Lieutenant, the space-suits are all tanked up?"

"Yes, sir." Indira's voice still had an icy edge to it. "The life-support systems are good for ten hours at maximum demand, the emergency systems will give two more hours, the jet-packs will allow ninety minutes of continuous manoeuvre."

"Well, then," said Conrad tranquilly, "the *Santa Maria,* as an aggressive mouse, is as ready as it ever will be to go and kick that sleeping elephant in the balls. It is my decision—which I have entered in the log—that the *Santa Maria* will match orbit and velocity with our enigmatic elephant. We will come up slowly and close, trying hard not to look aggressive in our intentions. While this is being done, we will continue trying to establish radio contact. If that does not succeed, at a range of twenty thousand metres we will try to make contact by visual signals. I have already instructed Matthew on the signalling procedure. And if that does not bring a response, we will nose in until we are close enough for me to jet across. I'll take a look around and maybe give the hull a few good kicks. And if that doesn't bring any reaction, I'll believe your theory, Kurt, that we have found a derelict."

"You think that is the wisest course, Commander?" Indira's voice indicated quite definitely that she thought his decision was stupid.

"You can suggest a better plan of action?" he countered.

"Why don't we ignore the bloody thing, touch down on Tantalus and carry out our proving programme?"

"Because, Lieutenant," he explained patiently, "we cannot afford to touch down without attempting to resolve this mystery. The moment we hit dirtside, the *Santa Maria* becomes a sitting duck. If that thing is occupied—and, for all I know, it may contain a thousand very aggressive little green men in S.A. all waiting for the alarm clock to say: Wake up, we're there—then we could have a nasty situation. Particularly if they think they have more right to colonise Tantalus than we have. Does that answer your question?"

"Yes, sir."

"I have a question, Boss," said Kwango.

"Go ahead. Spit it out."

"What happens if one of those little green men wakes up in time to notice your big hello. Suppose he is very irritable and goes: Bang, bang, you are dead."

"In that case you do not retaliate—I repeat, you do not retaliate. You get the hell out of it as fast as you can, if you can. If you can evade their detection equipment, you take the *Santa Maria* clean out of the Regulus system, put yourselves back in S.A. and report to Terra. Matthew is fully programmed for F.T.L. procedure. You would need something like six hours to get under way. If, on the other hand, the *Santa Maria* is attacked, you throw everything we have—such as it is—and still get out. O.K.?"

Kwango nodded. "It isn't going to come to that."

Conrad smiled. "Let us hope so. But if it does, you, Lieutenant Smith, will assume full command. It will be your responsibility to carry out these instructions as efficiently as possible. Understood?"

"Understood, Commander," Her voice had softened a little. "Don't make yourself a dead hero, that's all."

"I'll try not to . . . Now, let us all have a decent meal before we blast out of orbit."

Conrad waited until the alien vessel had passed over the night side of Tantalus and was approaching sunside before he made the rendezvous manoeuvres. The starship's computer would have carried out the operations perfectly; but Conrad preferred to control the *Santa Maria* himself. He prided himself on his skill as a space captain, and hated to think that a programmed machine could match his years of experience. One thing he knew intuitively—and derived some satisfaction from the knowledge—was that in an unanticipated crisis the man would make a sounder and faster decision than the machine.

The first power manoeuvre was carried out at one G acceleration, the second at two thirds G and the third at one third G. The *Santa Maria* edged cautiously towards the huge object.

Meanwhile, Luke continued to search the radio fre-

quencies and Matthew worked patiently through his sequence of variable pitch signals.

At a range of twenty thousand metres, the egg-shaped
object, brilliantly white in sunlight, looked awesome.

"Change now to visual signals, Matthew," said Conrad.
"Use the same sequence and try variable light intensities
and colours. Start at the red end of the spectrum, but
alternate with white light signals."

"Decision noted, Commander, Execution proceeds."

Kwango was looking through the manual telescope. "It's
got rows and rows of windows, Boss," he said excitedly.
"If those little green men are going to notice our existence,
now is the time."

"Not windows, port-holes," corrected Conrad absently.
"Any response, Matthew?" Now that was a bloody silly
question! The robot would have reported a response immediately.

"No response, Commander."

Kwango handed the telescope over to Indira. "I think
I can see things that might be radio antenna." she said
excitedly. "There are several rather thick spines sticking
out at regular intervals."

"Or they could be weapons," observed Conrad som-
berly. "I wish to hell we could get some kind of response.
The enigmatic silence doesn't give me a great feeling of
tranquillity."

Kwango laughed. "Would you feel any better if some
angry little character came on the vid, uttering gobbledy-
gook and making sinister gestures?"

"No. But at least I would know we had got through to
somebody . . . I am going down to the air-lock and
getting into a suit. If there is still no response by the time

I have hooked up all my gear, I'll take the *Santa Maria* in to one thousand metres range—very slowly. Then I will jet across and have a look-see . . . Matthew have one of your boys set up cameras to tape the whole approach operation."

"Decision noted, Commander. Execution proceeds."

Kwango said: "Why not send me across to that thing, Boss? Putting modesty aside, we both know I have a better computer between my ears than you have. But, apart from that, I am probably a shade more expendable. If there is something nasty in the woodshed, you are the guy who stands the best chance of getting this outfit back to Terra."

Conrad smiled. "Putting modesty aside, Kurt, I would love to send you—for three reasons: one, because I am a devout coward; two, because you have the better computer; and three, because you talk too much. But there is a problem. Dirtside, you are a genius. Spaceside, you are a babe in arms. I am a spaceman, you are not. And, despite your superior I.Q., if you tried to jet across to that vessel, you would be spinning arse over apex until your superior computer was a dizzy wreck. Does that answer your question?"

"Sorry, Commander. Will you accept a draw?" It was a reference to the last time Conrad and Kwango had played chess. Kwango had thought that he was in an impregnable position. But Conrad, sacrificing a bishop and a rook, had finally checkmated him with a queen supported by a pawn.

"No, Kurt. It's a resigning position—for you."

"What are you two talking about?" asked Indira.

"A game," said Kwango.

"A war game," amended Conrad. "Don't forget your orders. It is your task to get the *Santa Maria* back to Earth if I have the misfortune to make a one-way trip."

Phase Four

ENIGMA VARIATION THE FIRST

Conrad checked his equipment—the suit transceiver; the life-support pack; the reel of nylon thread; the electro-chron, thermometer, pressure metre, jet-fuel supply metre and air-mix indicator set in a thin strip of tungsten steel on the left forearm of his suit; and the laser torch.

There were two thousand metres of thread on the reel. It had a breaking point of one tonne. It was his life-line and death-line to the *Santa Maria* if jets failed, or if he was injured, or if his body was to be recovered. He slipped the loop on the end of the nylon thread into the feed slot of the Dead Man's Winder by the external door of the air-lock. A white light signalled that it was engaged. In the event of a disaster, he could be wound back to the *Santa Maria* at twenty k.p.h. He hoped it would not come to that.

He tested his suit jets. They worked perfectly. For a few seconds he jetted around in the airlock chamber, getting the feel of them once more. It had been a long time since he had used suit jets. But it was like riding an antique bicycle. Once you had the knack, you never lost it. Finally, he was satisfied. He signalled the nav deck.

"All systems go. I am now about to open the air-lock and jet over."

"Still no response," reported Kwango. "That thing is as dead as a dodo. Good luck, Boss."

"Thanks."

"Be very careful, James," said Indira.

He was glad she had called him James, and knew why.

It was on the tip of his tongue to tell her that the only living spacemen were the careful ones; but he thought better of it. "I'll be extremely careful," he assured her. Then he added softly: "Remember Applecross." Applecross was the place to which he had once taken her in the North West Highlands of Scotland. It had been a lovely interlude. And it seemed a long time ago.

"I was afraid you might have forgotten it," she said.

"No chance. That was one of the golden times . . . Over and out."

He de-pressurised the air-lock, comparing his own pressure metre with the one on the bulkhead. Both registered the fall identically. When the chamber was evacuated, he pressed the stud that operated the entry-port. The steel panel slid smoothly to one side.

Conrad jetted out into space. He glanced around him at the vast wilderness of stars, remote, diamond-sharp, beautiful. James Conrad was a hardened atheist; but when he was alone in space, he always experienced a strange impulse to pray. Not because he was afraid, but because he was always overwhelmed by the sheer splendour of the cosmos.

He glanced back at the *Santa Maria,* now some hundred meters away, taking care not to turn his visor toward Regulus. Not that it was too dangerous to glance at the brilliant sun. The phototropic visor would react instantly to its radiation, darkening to shut out the glare. But, when he turned away, the visor would take a second or two to become completely translucent once more. He did not want to be partly blind even for a couple of seconds.

He gazed at the vessel ahead. It was so vast that he felt as if he were an insect—a tiny fly buzzing towards a huge piece of cheese. He took one more look at the *Santa Maria*. Once it had seemed to him to be a massive vessel; but, compared to the alien ship, it was like a toy.

Sunlight caught the nylon thread connecting him to the *Santa Maria*. He felt for a moment as if he were some strange, armoured spider spinning a long tenuous strand. Then he put such fanciful notions out of his head and concentrated on the alien vessel, now only about five hundred metres away. He gave a small retro-blast on his suit jet to slow himself down. He wanted to arrive slowly, very slowly—not like a guided missile, more like a feather drifting.

Kwango's voice came over the radio. "How goes it, Boss?"

"Well enough, I'm going dead slow from here on. I don't want to excite anybody, and I want a good look at the ship before I touch down."

"You won't be exciting anybody—except, of course, the good Lieutenant Smith, who is discreetly biting her finger nails. That thing is dead, Commander. Matthew says so, the computer says so, and—most important of all, I say so. You have bought yourself a mausoleum."

"Thanks, Kurt. But don't forget to hit the D.M.W. button if the mausoleum yields up ghosts."

There was a chuckle. "Lieutenant Smith already has one finger poised. If she sneezes, you'll be hauled back so fast you'll spread like jam on impact. Over and out."

"Over and out."

Two hundred metres. Conrad gave another retro-blast. He wanted time to study the thing.

It was huge.

It filled him with awe.

It made him feel humble and insignificant.

Whatever race had built the vessel must have been far, far ahead of mankind in science and technology, even if it was not an F.T.L. ship.

Conrad allowed himself to drift slowly on, studying the details of the hull. The port-holes were about one metre in diameter, he judged. The transparent "glass" flashed annoyingly as it caught the sunlight. At fifty metres, he tried very hard to peer through one of the port-holes; but the reflected light stopped him. He would have a better chance when he touched down.

The rods projecting from the hull were of two kinds. One type was about two metres long and appeared to be hollow, the other type was about half a metre less and seemed solid. At various points along the hull there were large, hexagonal indentations. Conrad could not make up his mind about the function of the rods. They could be part of a system of telecommunications, they could be some kind of weapons—which he doubted—or they could belong to an energy dispersal system. Assuming the vessel was powered by nuclear reactors, that seemed the most likely explanation. But he was fairly confident that he knew the purpose of the hexagonal indentations. They were some three metres in diameter, and they were probably airlock entry ports.

At twenty metres, he was able to see that the hull—which before had seemed perfectly smooth—was pitted and scarred. Evidently, it had endured much bombardment from tiny meteors and other minute flotsam of space. Which argued that it had been around for a long time. A very long time.

Gently he drifted a few more metres, then expertly

reversed his attitude so that he could make contact feet first. He hoped the hull was of steel so that his magnetic boots would give him stability.

But the hull was not made of steel. He hit it lightly and bounced off. He had to use the vertical stabilisation jet on top of his head-piece to get him down and make him stay down. Which was a pity, because constant use of the stabilisation jet would decrease the time available for power manoevres.

Well, if the hull wasn't steel it was probably titanium. In the Solar System, titanium was very expensive and not very plentiful. Maybe in the system where this vessel had originated, titanium was the cheap metal and iron the costly one.

He made radio contact with the *Santa Maria*. "I have arrived safely. No problems, no signs of life."

"So we have observed," replied Kwango. "What are your intentions, Commander?"

"I'm going to kick on the hull. Somehow I don't think I'm going to see any curious face peering through the portholes. But first I'll try to look inside. I don't think I shall see much . . . The power system probably folded long ago . . . The skin of this thing isn't steel—I can't use my magnetic soles and I'm having to use the vertical jet to keep me down. I think it may be made of titanium. Anyway, it's been around a bloody long time. There are lots of typical micro-meteor scorings all over it . . . I've noticed a number of hexagonal markings that look as if they might be air-locks. If I can't kick any response out of the vessel, I'll torch my way through one of the air-locks."

"O.K., Boss. Take it easy. Lieutenant Smith is still hypnotised by the D.M.W. button."

Indira came in. "If it is dead, James, why not just leave it?"

"Because we need to find out why it was here—if we can. We need to find out what kind of people operated it and whether they could have any possible connection with the rings of Tantalus. Over and out."

Conrad walked carefully to the nearest port-hole. He peered through the "glass" and saw nothing but blackness —as he had expected. He straightened up and stamped heavily on the hull. The force of the action—despite the thrust of his vertical jet—lifted him three metres clear of the hull. He came back and stamped again, with the same result. He went through the procedure four times. Then he peered once more through a port-hole. There was nothing to be seen.

He reported back to the *Santa Maria*. "I've had enough of being a yo-yo. I'm going to torch my way in. If the metal is titanium it should not take too long."

Cautiously, he made his way to the nearest air-lock—if, indeed, that was what they were. He took care not to pass near any of the metal rods. It was almost certain that there were no living creatures on the ship. But it was still possible that the rods could discharge some sort of energy.

"Why not burn through one of the port-holes?" suggested Kwango. "It would probably be easier."

Conrad was professionally shocked. "Suppose we were in S.A. on the *Santa Maria* and somebody torched through to the nav deck. We'd all be dead of explosive decompression. We have a fail-safe on our air-lock. I assume these people have one on theirs."

Kwango chuckled. "Boss, you are a real white man."

"I'm a tresspasser," retorted Conrad primly. "I'm just trying to be as careful as I can."

The nearest hexagon was about one hundred and fifty metres from where Conrad had first touched down. He examined it carefully, and was none the wiser. It had to be an air-lock; but there was no way of knowing.

He unhooked the laser torch from his belt and set it at maximum power. "If t'were done," he quoted to himself, "t'were best done quickly." He had forgotten the reference, but he thought it was Shakespeare and—vaguely—Macbeth.

"How's that again, Boss?" asked Kwango.

"Nothing. I was talking to myself. Cancel statement."

Kwango did his impersonation of Matthew. "Decision noted. Execution proceeds."

From the way the laser torch sliced through the metal, it looked as if Conrad had been right about titanium. He cut a circular hole almost a metre in diameter. He needed it that big to get through without damaging his life-support systems.

As soon as the torch burned through the metal, Conrad braced himself. He had suspected that the lock might be filled with air. In which case, he would have been blasted away from the vessel as it rushed out.

He was right about it being an air-lock. He was wrong about it containing any air.

When there remained only two or three millimetres of metal left to be torched before he completed the full circle, Conrad killed the laser and returned the torch to his belt. Expertly, he tapped the section. It fell inside the lock. He adjusted his jets, switched on his head light, and went in after it.

The lock was not greatly dissimilar from the *Santa Maria*'s air-lock. It was a cubiform chamber; and Conrad was mystified as to why it should have a hexagonal exterior panel. Perhaps the hexagon had some emotive/intellectual/religious/philosophical/scientific significance for the people who designed it.

There was a problem, and it was a nasty one. The air-lock contained a control panel—as did the air-lock of the *Santa Maria*. But Conrad could not interpret the symbols. The problem was: should he torch his way through the panel that gave access to the vessel's interior, or should he pull out—having satisfied himself beyond any reasonable doubt that the vessel was derelict?

Indira's voice came over the radio. "Are you all right, James?"

"Yes. I'm in one of the air-locks. I'm afraid I am going to have to cut through into the main section of the ship, after all."

"Why not leave it and come back? You have proved that the thing is dead."

"All we know is that nobody has responded," he said. "We can't continue the Tantalus mission until we are sure there can be no interference from upstairs. I hate to have to do it, but I think I'm going to burn through."

"Then take care—and come back in one piece." She managed to laugh. "Kurt will testify that I am no longer hovering over the D.M.W. stud."

"That's right, Boss," cut in Kwango. "The Lieutenant is only looking pale and interesting."

"Fine. I'll keep you informed," said Conrad.

First he played with a series of buttons on what was evidently a control console. Nothing happened. Regretfully, he unhooked his laser torch and went to work once more.

He torched his way through the inner door much faster than he had managed to burn through the hull metal—which was hardly surprising.

Again, there was no outward blast of escaping air. He was profoundly grateful. If his action had evacuated the ship, he would have regarded himself as a homicidal—or would it be aliencidal?—vandal.

He jetted through the opening and found himself in a long, totally black corridor. Obviously, power systems were stone cold dead as, most likely, was everything else.

He let his headlight play along the corridor in both directions. There seemed to be no end to it.

"I designate the fat end of this vessel as north and the small end as south," he reported back. "I am in a long north-south corridor. I am jetting north to see what I can see."

He adjusted his jets and began to move. He had gone about two hundred and fifty metres when he came upon an amazing sight.

The corridor led to a wide railed causeway or ledge that ran round an immense chamber. The chamber contained the twisted and shattered remains of a great deal of intricate machinery. Though he did not recognise the function of the fragmented equipment, Conrad surmised that he was in the engine-room.

He peered "down" into the well of the chamber—and saw stars.

He saw stars through a jagged hole, some thirty metres across, in the vessel's hull. The torn metal edges of the skin were bent inwards as if the hull had been pierced by a missile of some kind. He looked up—and again saw stars.

There was a corresponding hole directly above—the exit hole. There, the ripped metal plate was bent outwards. But the shape and size of the tear was about the same.

He held on to the "hand" rail to stop himself drifting, and stayed there, marvelling at the sight for some minutes. He was awed and saddened by what he saw. This fantastic vessel had doubtless travelled through the light-years with a huge complement and/or huge pay-load only to meet with the kind of catastrophe that haunts the dreams of all spacemen.

Kwango's voice broke the spell. "Commander, you all right?"

Conrad shook himself out of his reverie. For all he knew, the disaster had happened thousands of years ago; but the sense of tragedy was timeless.

"Yes, I'm all right. This vessel presents no threat. Something—or someone—has punched a bloody great hole —two bloody great holes—through its vitals . . . I'd like to explore it thoroughly. But if I get drawn into that caper, we are going to lose a lot of precious time. U.N. is paying us to prove Tantalus. Now that I have satisfied myself that this thing is harmless, we'll get on with our work. If Tantalus doesn't turn out to be too rough, and if any potential saboteurs don't start tossing spanners when we are not looking, maybe there will be the opportunity to come upstairs again."

Kwango laughed. "Or the horse may talk," he said obscurely.

"What the hell does that mean?"

"Nothing, Boss. Just a private joke."

Conrad glanced once more at the scene of desolation. "Tell the joke, Kurt. I'm in a mood for funnies."

"O.K. Boss. Several centuries ago, there was this King Louis of France, which is a country on that offshore island to Britain they call Eurasia. Well, King Louis had heard there was some guy who had the fluence and could make animals speak. Louis didn't believe this too much, but he had a favourite horse and he thought it would be fun to hear its opinions about this and that. So he had this guy brought to him and said: They tell me you make animals talk. Make my horse talk. How much time do you need?

"Now this guy knew he didn't really have the fluence. But he was afraid the king might get real mad if he confessed. So he said: I need one year, Majesty.

"Hokay, said the king. One year it is. If the horse talks you hit the jack-pot. If it doesn't you are in dead trouble. And how do you like that?

"When the king had dismissed him, this guy went home and told his buddy about the situation. The buddy was all shook up. He said: Look, friend, I know you can't do it, and you know you can't do it. The shit is going to hit the fan. But the guy who was supposed to have the fluence gave a big smile and said: A lot can happen in a year, friend. I may die, or Louis may die—or the horse may talk."

Conrad laughed. "I take the point. We have one planetary cycle to prove Tantalus."

"That's it, Boss. And if we don't get knocked off, let us hope the horse talks."

"Get some lager nice and cool. I'm jetting back . . . And get Matthew to start the resuscitation sequences for Khelad, Uhlmann and Zonis—in that order. Now we know we are not going to be zapped by an alien egg, we had

better try to find out which—if any—of our chilled comrades harbours animosity."

"Decision noted," said Kwango. "Execution proceeds."

ENIGMA VARIATION THE SECOND

The six Expendables were in the *Santa Maria*'s saloon. The meal had been excellent, and Conrad has ensured that plenty of wine and spirits were available. He wanted everyone—particularly the three who had recently emerged from suspended animation—to feel relaxed. He noted with relief that Ahmed Khelad, though a Muslim, was not averse to alcohol. If Khelad was the bad boy, booze might relax him sufficiently to make a small mistake.

"I give you a toast," said Conrad. "Let us drink to Alexei, who will take—as they say—new heart when we touch down on Tantalus and Lieutenant Smith can operate."

"To Alexei!" Everyone drank, and everyone was slightly smashed. But Conrad was not too smashed to notice that Ruth Zonis managed to squirt most of her brandy over her face. There were roars of laughter. Khelad, on the other hand, took his brandy like a spaceman to the manner born. Lisa Uhlmann swallowed hers with ferocious intensity.

"Ahmed," Conrad affected surprise, "I thought your religion forbade the taking of liquor."

Khelad smiled. "Allah has given me a special dispensation. I shall not be denied my quota of houris in Paradise."

"I presume the dispensation is for services rendered—or about to be rendered."

"Yes, effendi. For services rendered or about to be rendered."

Ahmed Khelad was slender, wiry, good-looking. No doubt, thought Conrad, he could be a big hit with women —when he wanted to be.

"Some of your fellow Arabs are not as broadminded as you, Ahmed," said Conrad. "Not only do they stick to the letter of the Koran, but they disapprove of new worlds being opened up for mankind. They think the money should be spent raising their standard of living."

Khelad shrugged. "It is a point of view . . . You must know, Commander, that many of the peoples of Islam are conservative in their ideas. That is not, perhaps, an entirely bad thing."

Ruth Zonis was either very pissed or very good at seeming to be very pissed. She tossed her long, black hair and gazed at Khelad with wide expressive eyes. "We know all about the conservative attitudes of the Arabs," she said thickly. "For centuries your people marked time. They did little or nothing with their land and little or nothing with their culture. Then, when Israel started to turn the desert green, your Islamic friends got all hot and bothered. They tried to push the Israelis into the sea and turn fertile land back into desert." She laughed. "It was a big mistake. You only outnumbered us ten to one. So there was no real problem."

Ahmed gazed at her coolly. "That is ancient history. We have all progressed since then. Ruth, you are beautiful, you are intelligent, and you are a Jewess. I have no quarrel with you. I will drink to the future of Israel. Is that enough to make us friends?"

Zonis raised her glass also. "It is enough to stop us being enemies."

Lisa Uhlmann said: "You are not being very gracious, Ruth. Let us drink also to all Third World countries—which have been used as pawns for too long in the interminable chess game between the U.S.A. and the Soviet Union."

Conrad glanced at Lieutenant Smith and Kwango. Indira, one eyebrow raised, was looking at Lisa Uhlmann. Kwango looked benignly at Khelad.

"My great-great grandfather's ghost," said Kwango, "has just reminded me that the Arabs once sold my people into slavery."

"That is perfectly true, Kurt," said Ahmed. "It is also true that Commander Conrad's ancestors exploited my people, your people, and Lieutenant Smith's people. Can we not forget the past?"

Conrad saw that tempers were rising. Should he cool it or not cool it? He decided to cool it. Surely any potential saboteur was not going to allow himself or herself to be exposed by taunting.

"I'm about to play the heavy," he said. "All previous statements are cancelled. The message is this: we are all human beings, and our task is to prove Tantalus fit for colonization by human beings, whether they are Israeli, Arab, Negro, Indian or whatever. So the final toast is mankind—may it flourish and prosper . . . And after you have squirted the last of the brandy, kindly remember that you are all Expendables. We are going to prove this planet. Some of us may die in the process. But we are going to score for stupid old *homo sapiens*."

"I'll drink to stupid old *homo sapiens*," said Lieutenant

Smith. "He may come in assorted colours and sizes, but his blood is always red."

Conrad finished his brandy. "Now, I'll tell you why we have had this extra booze ration. We are going to begin to work good and hard. Khelad, Zonis and Uhlmann have been out of S.A. long enough to adjust. As you know, while you were still in the cooler, we discovered the existence of this huge derelict vessel and had to use some previous time proving it represented no threat. However the fact that it was holed by something big gives cause for concern. It is remotely possible that the missile originated on Tantalus. The information the robot probe brought back to Earth is not sufficient to preclude this idea. All it told us was that Tantalus is Earth-type, with an Earth-type biosphere based on the carbon cycle and with an oxygen-nitrogen atmosphere. The data the probe gave up suggested—but did not prove—that there was no technologically-based civilization. No radio emissions were registered, nor was there any indication of any kind of electric power or atomic energy. The probe could not even determine what substance the rings were made of.

So we are left with this situation: there is in eccentric orbit one vast disabled star-ship, dirtside there are five enigmatic rings, each about five kilometres in diameter, horizontally placed in a kind of clearing, geometrically related to each other in an exact pentagon on Continent A. Continent B has no rings. Continent C has no rings. The numerous islands and archipelagos have no rings . . . So, before we touch down on Continent A to investigate the ring system, we are going into low-level orbit. We are going to check and recheck the data given by the probe.

"Six hours from now, I intend to transfer the *Santa Maria* from its present one thousand kilometres orbit to an orbit of two hundred and fifty kilometres altitude. The vessel will be skating just above the extreme limits of the atmosphere, so we shall not be able to stay long without further power manoeuvres.

"I anticipate remaining in the two-fifty slot for about twenty orbits. During that time we will exercise full telemetry and we will also have two people constantly on watch on the nav deck. Three of us are veterans, three of us are newcomers. We will pair appropriately. I will stand watch with Khelad. Lieutenant Smith will stand watch with Ulhmann. Kwango will stand watch with Zonis."

There was a brief silence. Then Ahmed Khelad said softly: "Commander, cannot the robots perform the routine task of observation?"

Conrad met his gaze. "No, Khelad. They will be concerned with telemetry and the safety of the vessel. Also, we need to form our own impression of the world we are about to invade."

ISRAELI LOGIC

The *Santa Maria* had completed twenty-five orbits when Conrad decided that it was time to touch-down. During that time, he had worked the new Expendables hard. Apart from keeping watch and taking strenuous exercise in the workout chamber, then had to collate and interpret the data supplied by the magnetometric, infra-red and telephoto search systems. Deliberately and systematically, he irritated them by making them carry out tasks that could have been accomplished faster and more efficiently by the computer or even by the robots. When Uhlmann protested, he piled on the pressure, inventing useless routine checks and going through all the safety drill procedures that had been built in as conditioned reflexes in the basic training programme back on Terra.

He did not spare himself or Lieutenant Smith or Kwango, since it was necessary to keep the others under continuous surveillance.

At length, after poring for what seemed like endless hours over magnetometric print-out that the computer would have interpreted in minutes, Ruth Zonis, red-eyed, came to the nav deck while Conrad and Khelad were on watch.

"May I have a private talk with you, Commander?"

"Is it likely to take long?" Conrad glanced through the nav deck observation panel. The *Santa Maria* was passing over nightside. There was little to be seen with the naked eye except the faint glow of moonlight on great oceans, between the whorls of cloud formations. But the infra-red monitor showed a radically different picture.

"I don't think so."

Conrad turned to Khelad. "How about stretching your legs for five minutes, Ahmed. O.K.?"

"O.K., Commander." He smiled at Ruth Zonis. "I hope you are not breaking up, Ruth. It's a tough programme the Commander has devised for us. Something tells me it may get even harder."

"Israelis do not break very easily," she retorted. "You, of all people, should know that."

Expertly, he walked across the bond-fuzz carpeting. Khelad was proud of the fact that he was the best of the new recruits at operating in zero gravity. While the others sometimes trod too heavily on the hooked fibres and, as a result, bounced up to drift helplessly, Ahmed seemed to have the natural aptitude of the spaceman. The soles of his shoes engaged perfectly wherever he trod.

When he had left the nav deck, Conrad said: "What is your problem, Zonis?"

"You are working us very hard, Commander. Too hard. I have a theory that you are trying to break us—or, at least, to break one of us."

"Why should I do that?"

"Because you are afraid that the team may contain a saboteur."

Conrad was silent for a few seconds. "Do you have any special reason for making that statement?"

"It's true, isn't it?"

"Zonis, you are answering a question with another question."

She shrugged. "I'm sorry. But I am not oblivious of Third World politics, Commander. I also know that you are making us carry out many needless and strenuous duties. You are driving us to the point of exhaustion. There has to be a reason. I think I know it."

"Assuming your hypothesis is correct, do you also know who the potential saboteur may be?"

Ruth Zonis smiled. "I know it is not me—but I can't prove that to you, of course. I don't think it is Alexei Pushkin, because you have left him in the cooler—for reasons that may or may not be valid—and he doesn't have to take part in the obstacle race. So it has to be either Khelad or Uhlmann. It could be Lisa, but I am betting on Khelad."

"Ahmed has performed all his duties perfectly," retorted Conrad. "I have no cause for complaint."

"He is pretty good," conceded Zonis. "Also, he is the perfect diplomat. I have tried to make him lose his cool, but I can't . . . Isn't that what you would expect from a well-trained saboteur?"

"I might also expect a well-trained saboteur to make the statements you have just made."

"You can't watch all of us all the time, Commander. You will have to trust somebody, otherwise you are not going to be able to prove Tantalus."

"You think I should trust you?"

She nodded. "I think I am a logical choice."

"I am aware of your record. The last time we all ate together in the saloon, you were deliberately trying to provoke Khelad."

"As I said, I thought he might just possibly flip and betray himself."

"But he didn't. Maybe because he is a well-trained

saboteur. Maybe just because he is an intelligent man . . .
Anyway, you will be relieved to know, Zonis, that after
five more orbits we are going dirtside. We'll see what
Tantalus has to offer."

She sighed. "You aren't going to trust me, are you?"

"No more than I have to. And that goes for everyone
. . . You and your friends were playing some very compli-
cated games when you raided Cairo Museum. If you had
succeeded in your plans, the ExPEND programme would
have been at risk."

Ruth Zonis looked startled. "I didn't think of it like
that."

"I did," said Conrad drily. "This discussion is termi-
nated. Tell Khelad he can return to duty."

When Ahmed Khelad returned to the nav deck, he said:
"Has the pretty little Jewess been telling tales about me,
Commander?"

"Khelad, the discussion was and remains private."

"Sorry, Commander. Maybe we'll lose this Arab-Israeli
thing on Tantalus. I like Ruth. She is a woman of spirit."

"I have read my history," said Conrad. "I think I have
learned why Arabs like women of spirit."

Stage Two

TOUCH-DOWN

Phase One

TOUCH-DOWN AND EVALUATIONS

When the rockets died, there was a great stillness. The *Santa Maria* had touched down about twenty-five kilometres south of the ring complex. Everyone began to fumble at the straps of their contour-berths on the navigation deck.

Conrad, space veteran that he was, made every movement slowly and deliberately, giving his limbs time to adjust to a gravity that was more than ninety per cent as strong as that of Terra.

Uhlmann and Khelad fairly leaped out of their contour-berths—and fell flat on their faces.

Conrad gazed down at them benignly. "More haste, less speed. Your muscles are in lousy shape. All our muscles are in lousy shape. We are all going to have to tone them up before we get out of the air-lock."

Kwango got out of his berth without any difficulty. "O.K. if I roll back the screen and take a look through the observation panel, Commander?"

"In a minute, Kurt. General orders first. The day on Tantalus lasts twenty-three hours seven minutes, Standard Earth Time. While the robots make preliminary surveys of our immediate vicinity, we will get ourselves back to a state of operational efficiency in a fairly strong G field. Lieutenant Smith, you will look to the welfare of Alexei Pushkin. I want him operational as soon as possible."

"Yes, Commander. You are not forgetting that . . ." She left the sentence unfinished.

"No, I am not forgetting anything." He gazed at the six Expendables calmly. "There is nothing wrong—at least, I hope there is nothing wrong—with Alexei Pushkin's heart. I kept him in the cooler deliberately. According to my information, it is possible that we have a saboteur on board the *Santa Maria*. It cannot be myself for obvious reasons. Nor can it be Lieutenant Smith or Kurt Kwango for the same reasons. It could be one of you. Or it could be Pushkin. I have, as you know, six robots at my command. Normally they are programmed not to be able to harm human beings. I have changed that programme and have inserted homicidal capability. Three of the robots will be on permanent duty in sensitive areas of this vessel until I am satisfied that there is no saboteur—which I hope—or that he or she has been discovered.

"This will undoubtedly place some strain on our exploration capacity. But I think we can cope."

He glanced searchingly at Khelad, Uhlmann and Zonis. "I greatly hope that none of you wants to wreck this mission. On the assumption that you all may be entirely innocent, I apologise in advance for the surveillance and restrictions that are obviously necessary. None of you— Pushkin included—will be allowed access to the following areas unless accompanied by Lieutenant Smith, Kwango or myself: the nav deck, the engine-room, the weapons and stores hold, the laboratory, the computer room. When we begin the exploration programme, we will operate in pairs. Weapons and explosives will only be issued on my authority. The robots Matthew, Mark and Luke will be available to assist our efforts at exploration and proving. John, Peter and Paul are the Praetorian guard and will not leave their posts until we have resolved this problem, one way or another. Now, let's all take a look through the observation panel. One day—if we can do a good job—Tantalus may support one thousand million human beings. If we have a saboteur, let him weigh the value of his own cause against the value of that. Message ends."

"This is monstrous!" said Lisa Uhlmann. "How can we give our best if we are under suspicion and constantly watched?"

Conrad shrugged. "I cannot recall promising you an easy life when you volunteered to join the Expendables."

"So I was right," said Ruth Zonis. "You were hoping to make the saboteur betray himself when we were in orbit."

"It was a gambit," admitted Conrad. "Not a strong one, but worth trying."

Khelad smiled. "Commander, permit me to congratulate you. In your position, I would do exactly the same."

"Would you, Ahmed? That is interesting."

Kwango had rolled back the screen. The observation panel revealed the surface of Tantalus from a height of ninety metres. It was impossible to look straight down; but the panel revealed a broad expanse of grassland. In the middle distance there was the beginning of a semi-tropical forest and, far beyond that and misty in the far distance, a range of snow-capped mountains. The blue sky was flecked with cloud, and the sun had passed its zenith. Local time, it was mid-afternoon.

Kwango peered through the manual telescope. "Ever been to Kenya, Commander? It is in Africa. This place reminds me of it very much."

"No, I haven't ever been to Kenya, but I do know it is in Africa . . . Any sign of animal life?"

Kwango shrugged. "No. But that means nothing. Anything within a radius of twenty-five kilometres and possessing a central nervous system must have shit itself stupid when we came roaring out of the sky."

"Take a good look, everyone," said Conrad. "This is the world we are going to prove for human colonisation."

"It looks very ordinary, very Earth-like," said Lieutenant Smith.

"So did Kratos," said Conrad, "and that gave us some very interesting moments."

"Where is the ring system?"

"Planetary north. Twenty-five or thirty kilometres inside that forest. If the rings were fabricated by intelligent beings, and if said intelligtnt beings are still around, they will be aware of our coming."

Matthew came to the navigation deck. "Engine-room and control systems checked, Commander. All propulsion systems closed down. Power systems normal. Slight malfunction in re-cycling unit now being repaired."

"Good. John, Peter and Paul are at their stations?"

Matthew contrived to sound pained. "Your decisions are always executed, Commander."

Conrad scratched his silver eye-patch irritably. He was aware that it was a mannerism that was becoming more and more frequent. He made a mental note to try and stop it.

"Cancel query."

"Decision noted. Execution proceeds."

"These are my further instructions. You will assign the two remaining robots to immediate external survey. They will inspect the landing torus for possible damage, determine the attitude of this vessel and report back. If no damage and if altitude is less than five degrees from vertical, they will proceed as follows: one, they will set

up four vid cameras north, south, east, west at a distance
of fifty metres from the *Santa Maria*; two, they will test
hook-in to command screens; three, they will collect soil,
air, vegetation specimens and return same to air-lock for
analysis; four, they will sweep an area of one thousand
metres radius from this vessel; five, if animal life-forms
are encountered, the robots will transfer visual data to
command screen one; six, if hostile life-forms are encountered, the robots will return to *Santa Maria* at maximum speed without accepting any risk or taking any re-
taliatory measures. Execute."

"Decisions noted, Commander. Execution proceeds.
Mark and Luke are now assembling their equipment in
the air-lock. Estimated time for transfer of equipment
dirtside, eleven point five minutes. Estimated time for
immediate external survey, four point—"

"Data not required," snapped Conrad irritably. "Execute
with maximum efficiency, that is all."

"All operations are carried out with maximum efficiency,
sir. In case of malfunction in any other robot, my command circuit can override—"

"I know about your command circuits. Cancel statement."

"Decision noted. Execution proceeds."

Phase Two

TALE OF A PREHENSILE TAIL

The *Santa Maria* had not damaged itself on touch-down and the distortion of the large landing torus was negligible. Some of the titanium cladding had been dented but not even badly enough to justify repair. The ship's attitude was slightly over three degrees from the vertical, which was nothing at all to worry about.

When the robots had reported and Conrad was satisfied about the safety of his vessel, they proceeded to carry out their other tasks. The vid cameras were set on tripods, each with a variable speed rotating mechanism to support the head. Conrad ordered the north and south cameras to be set on one-minute rotation and the east and west cameras on two-minute rotation. But each camera could also be independently controlled from the command screens on the nav deck. Thus the immediate vicinity of the ship could be under constant surveillance.

The samples collected by the robots were surprising only in their remarkable ordinariness. They were analysed by Ruth Zonis and Lisa Uhlmann under the watchful eyes of Kwango. The air was oxygen/nitrogen in a rich 76/24 proportion. There were traces of argon, neon, helium, zenon and krypton—as in the air of Terra. Uhlmann was amazed at the similarity.

"This is astounding," she said to no one in particular.

"The air of Tantalus is actually better for us than the air of Earth."

Kwango yawned. "Lisa, after proving Kratos, I am almost immune to wonder. Not entirely, just almost. I have a notion that Tantalus is too good to be true."

"What do you mean by that?"

The big negro laughed and flexed his muscles. "It seems to be a place where every prospect pleases . . . Do you know the rest of the quotation?"

Lisa Uhlmann stood up and stretched, thrusting out her breasts. They were very good breasts, Kwango noted. Some day, he thought, if she is not the one who is trying to blow us all, I'll try for a more intimate examination of those tits.

"Where every prospect pleases," said Lisa, observing the way he looked at her, "and man alone is vile."

Kwango laughed. "Score one."

"I score two. You fancy me."

"Yes," agreed Kwango. "I fancy you. But score one only. Until I and the good Commander are satisfied that you are not going to be naughty, score one. Your breasts do not carry a written guarantee of loyalty."

Lisa Uhlmann shrugged. "Nevertheless, I am a damn good chemist, Kurt."

"So you are. You have yet to prove that you are a damn good Expendable."

Ruth Zonis worked efficiently and enthusiastically. The soil of Tantalus was a dark, heavy loam, rich in organic matter—far richer than the almost worn-out soil of Earth that had had to yield too many crops to support too many people, and was now paying the price for having been boosted for one and a half centuries by chemical fertilisers. She found nitrogen-fixing bacteria in plenty on the roots

of a small plant that greatly resembled terrestrial clover.
She isolated tiny insects and prepared them for micro-
scopic examination. She even found a worm.

"Kurt, Lisa! This soil is so rich we could grow anything.
We have hit the jackpot. We have come to a biological
wonderland."

"Then," retorted Kwango tranquilly, "all we have to do
is take the joker out of the pack, and *homo sapiens* will
have another planet to mess up."

"The joker being our real or imagined saboteur?"

"The joker is the joker," said Kwango.

Meanwhile, Alexei Pushkin was being brought out of
suspended animation. Matthew was the star performer.
Matthew with his thermal gloves and his unfailing efficiency. Lieutenant Smith was merely an observer. Medi-
cally, there was no need for her presence. She did not even
need to supervise. Matthew's skill was irreproachable.

But she knew why Conrad really wanted her to be
there. There was just a chance that, when he came out
of S.A., Alexei Pushkin might make some revealing utter-
ance before he was in full possession of his faculties.
Nothing he might say could establish that he was not a
saboteur. But he just might say something that would
prove his guilt.

Indira watched Matthew massage expertly with the
thermal gloves, bringing heat close to the heart. Alexei's
naked body seemed curiously shrunken. In life, he was a
big robust man: in suspended animation, he seemed small,
vulnerable, almost unimportant. S.A., thought Indira, was
a biological outrage. She knew it was necessary if mankind
was to get out to the stars. No one could consciously experience faster-than-light drive and remain sane. Only

robots could take the nightmarish stresses and remain rational; but that was because the robots had rigidly programmed logic circuits, and no emotional apparatus. They were programmed to ignore irrelevant data. Human beings could not be so programmed—thank God!

"How is Pushkin doing, Matthew?"

"Temperature is still three degrees Centigrade below independent life-support, Lieutenant. There is intermittent heart response; but the breathing cycle is not yet actuated. Condition normal for this stage. Estimated time for full resuscitation thirty-two minutes, S.E.T. If the situation is designated as an emergency, the time factor can be reduced to twenty-one minutes, but the risk of heart damage will be increased. Do you wish to designate emergency?"

"No, Matthew. Continue normal resuscitation."

"Decision noted. Execution proceeds."

While Matthew continued his thermal massage in the heart area, he placed his other thermal glove under the blue and shrunken testicles. They grew larger. The tiny protrusion of the penis expanded. Pushkin had an erection.

Indira smiled. As a doctor, she knew that frequently men at the point of death had erections. It was part of the biological programme, the indomitable will to survive and procreate. It was new to her that they also had erections when they were coming out of suspended animation. She was amused that the penis had begun to function before the lungs. Nature played strange tricks . . .

Twenty-seven minutes later, Alexei Pushkin screamed and tried to sit up. He saw a woman bending over him, and a monstrous metal thing with the word Matthew painted on its chest plate.

He said: "Tell them I'll do it! I want to do it!" Then he sank back and closed his eyes.

Matthew said: "Heart functions well, breathing cycle vigorous, disorientation normal for trauma of emergence."

Indira picked up Pushkin's hand and held it. The fingers were still chilled. Professionally, she felt his pulse. Pushkin's heart was beating vigorously. He gazed up at her as if he did not know her—which he did not, though presently he would. Coming out of S.A. almost invariably produced disorientation and temporary amnesia. But it soon passed.

"Shall I proceed with data feed?" enquired Matthew.

Indira smiled faintly. Data feed! What a hell of a phrase to describe the process of telling a traumatised man who he is, where he is, what he is.

"No, Matthew. I will give him the necessary information."

"Decision noted."

She looked down at Pushkin. With an effort, he focussed on her face.

"You are Alexei Pushkin," she said quietly, "and there is no need for anxiety. You are with friends and you are being looked after expertly. You have just emerged from suspended animation. You are in the star-ship *Santa Maria*, which has touched down safely on the planet Tantalus. You are the engineer in a team of Expendables whose task is to prove Tantalus fit for human colonisation. The team consists of seven men and women, and six robots. Do you wish to ask any questions?"

He was silent for a while, making a great effort to concentrate. Finally he said: "Who betrayed me?"

Lieutenant Smith gazed at him intently. "What was there to betray?"

He gave a dreadful laugh. "Do you think I am entirely stupid." Then he fainted. The pulse became weak.

Lieutenant Smith said: "I will use adrenalin."

Matthew was already filling the hypodermic syringe. "Decision noted," he said with what seemed the merest hint of sarcasm.

Lieutenant Smith attended to her patient.

Meanwhile, Conrad and Khelad were on the nav deck, sitting gazing at the screens hooked in to the external vid cameras. Occasionally one or other of them got up, stretched, walked about, took a look through the observation panel.

The two robots outside the vessel had already completed their one thousand metre search. They had discovered no large animal life-forms—which was not surprising. When the *Santa Maria* came roaring out of the sky, the shattering noise of its touch-down would have driven all intelligent life-forms away at a great rate of knots.

Now, the robots had been instructed to construct a perimeter defence system at a radius of one hundred metres from the vessel. It consisted of steel net, supported by light angle-girders driven into the ground. The fence was to be linked by a step-up transformer to the *Santa Maria's* generator. The fence would carry one thousand volts at low amperage. That would be sufficient power, thought Conrad, to discourage any but the most dedicated intruders.

On the screens, he checked the progress of the robots. It looked as if they would have the fence complete before darkness fell.

Khelad was pacing up and down nervously. Eventually he spoke: "Commander, I am not your saboteur. I cannot prove it, but it is so. I, too, want Tantalus for mankind. You must believe me."

Conrad did not take his gaze from the screens. Khelad's voice sounded very tight, he noted. That was good. Stress might make him careless.

"Ahmed, I am very glad that you say—with apparent conviction—that you are not a saboteur and that you want to prove Tantalus. Alas, it is my duty neither to believe you nor disbelieve you. You understand my position?"

"I do, sir."

"Good. Maybe we shall find the saboteur, maybe not. Maybe there is no saboteur. But, for the time being, all of the new recruits remain suspect."

"That is clearly necessary," conceded Khelad. "But as I am aware of my own innocence, I am in a better position than you, Commander. I can narrow the suspects down to two."

Conrad raised an eyebrow. "Three, surely? Assuming, of course, your own innocence."

"No, two. I have been thinking very carefully about Ruth Zonis. She had done her best to provoke me. If she were the saboteur, she would not do that. She would not wish to call attention to herself. Does that seem reasonable?"

"It does, Ahmed." He sighed. "But it is equally possible that the pair of you may be interested in creating a diversion."

Khelad looked startled. "What do you mean by that— sir?"

"You work it out. Meanwhile, take a spell at the screens while I stretch my legs."

Khelad took over. Conrad got up from his chair, rubbed the back of his neck and yawned.

After a time, Khelad said: "When will we be going

through the air-lock, Commander?"

"When Kwango has evaluated the lab reports and presented his findings . . . Tomorrow morning, I imagine."

"Do you have any theory about the rings, sir?"

Conrad shrugged. "None worth mentioning . . . But Kwango will have. That black bastard is our very own self-appointed think-tank. His arrogance, fortunately for him, is backed up by a high I.Q."

Kheland seemed surprised. "I did not think you would have any racial prejudice."

"Oh, but I have. I don't like Negroes, Arabs, Israelis, Americans, Russians. I don't even much care for the British. I have a very strong racial prejudice. It is in favour of the human race. Remember that."

Suddenly, Khelad shouted. "Look!"

Conrad whirled to face the screens. But he was too late.

"What did you see?"

"North camera. For a moment only. Range possibly two hundred metres. It was ape-like, humanoid—I don't know. But it had a prehensile tail."

Conrad gazed intently at the screens, but saw only the robots working methodically on the perimeter fence. The sky was blue, the sun was low. In the distance there were a few birds.

"How do you know it had a prehensile tail?"

"Because it was arched over the creature's head." Khelad's voice sounded almost hysterical. "Also, the tail seemed to have something like a hand on the end of it."

"It isn't there now."

Khelad pulled himself together, and looked somewhat embarrassed. "No, Commander, it isn't there now."

THE KWANGO SCENARIO

Conrad and Khelad watched the screens carefully while the light remained; but there was no further sign of the ape-like creature. If indeed it existed. Perhaps Khelad's suspiciously brief sighting was itself a diversionary tactic.

The robot Mark was ordered to set up a rotating search-light, while Luke took over on the nav deck for the long and monotonous night watch.

Conrad gave him precise instructions. "You will monitor all four screens. If any animal life-forms are revealed by the search-light you will simultaneously lock the light on target and record the sequence on videotape. If any such life-form is significantly large—defined as being at least one metre in height or one metre in length—you will signal my cabin. If any such life-form is observed in significant numbers—defined as any number greater than ten—you will signal general alarm. If Ahmed Khelad, Ruth Zonis or Lisa Uhlmann come to the navigation deck not escorted by me, or Lieutenant Smith or Kurt Kwango, you will also signal general alarm and you will restrain the intruder without injury until I arrive."

"Decisions noted, Commander. Execution proceeds."

That evening after dinner, Conrad asked Kwango to come to his cabin.

"Well, Kurt, give me the news . . . Would you like a drink?"

"It's real kind of de Massa Boss to drink wid dis pore black sinner. I sure could use a drop of de white ladies' ruin."

Conrad sighed. "Kurt, you really press your luck with this Uncle Tom stuff. One of these days, before I have time to realise I'm losing a good ecologist, I'll spread your brains all over the bulkhead."

Kwango took his drink and was instantly apologetic. "Sorry, Commander. It's stupid and I'm trying to kick it . . . High I.Q., low sense of humour . . . Compensation, or something like that."

"It figures," said Conrad. He took a swig of his own whiskey. "Now get sensible."

"The news is nothing but good. Zonis and Uhlmann have worked themselves into the deck analysing the samples. They have given me a lot of useful data; and, of course, when we are allowed outside, I'll have a lot more. Do you want to go through the data with me, or should I just boil it down."

"Boil it down. It's been a tiring day."

"O.K., Boss. It looks as though the biosphere of Tantalus is a natural paradise. The air is slightly richer in oxygen, and there is not the slightest trace of the Earth-type pollutants. Nobody has been fucking this planet about —and that's for sure. The soil samples are a farmer's dream—black prairie soil, rich in organic matter, non-saline, highly productive. We should be able to plough it up, toss in Earth seeds and jump back quickly so we won't get hit when the crop shoots up." Kwango gave a grim smile. "Be a long time before even greedy Earth men can turn this place into a dust-bowl. To sum up, it's as near as dammit like the temperate and semi-tropical regions of Earth about a hundred thousand years before some fool Terran discovered the use of fire."

"In short, the jackpot?"

"In short, the jackpot."

"Except, perhaps, for the rings."

"Except, perhaps, for the rings," agreed Kwango. "But I'm not worrying too much. I have my theories about those rings . . . We had it rough on Kratos, Commander, but we licked the death worms."

Conrad gave a faint smile. "What you really meant to say was that you licked the death worms."

"With some slight assistance," said Kwango generously.

"Your kami-kaze attack on the queen provided some useful data."

Conrad ignored the provocation. "Tell me the Kwango explanation of the riddle of the rings."

Kwango looked pained. "Boss, it's only a first scenario. I don't like to commit myself until I have some more data."

"Commit yourself, Kurt. That is an order."

Kwango sighed. "You are a hard man to work for, Commander."

"I know. Spill."

"Well, they are not the work of intelligent indigenes."

"Why not?"

"Because there ain't no intelligent indigenes. Or if there were, they have all gone under the hill."

"Why do you say that?"

"Orbital survey. No trace of nuclear power, no radio signals, no sign of electric power, no internal combustion engines, not even a puff of smoke from de ole steam engine. So, given the facts that we have one large moth-eaten derelict space vessel in eccentric orbit and that we also have a mute enigmatic ring system on Tantalus, the first Kwango scenario goes as follows: the space vessel brought an alien and intelligent life-form to Tantalus—probably for reasons similar to ours.

"Surprise, surprise! They found somebody had got here before them. The rings have to have a function. If they were the work of indigenes, there would probably be other systems all over the planet. So they were built by exploration group one for some as yet unknown reason."

"If they *were* built by natives," said Conrad, "they wouldn't necessarily have to be all over the planet. Take Earth. There's only one set of pyramids."

"Yes," countered Kwango, "but there are other types of monument to human stupidity. Here on Tantalus, there is nothing but the ring system . . . So the first Kwango scenario maintains that group one didn't give the big hello when group two arrived. Chances are, they blasted the starship before any of its crew could drop dirtside. What we have we hold, and all that crap. Not very nice people."

"So where are the descendants of group one?" demanded Conrad.

"I don't know, Boss," said Kwango weakly. "Maybe the star-ship took them out while it was getting hammered . . . I need more data."

"You also need your head examined. The odds against two groups from different parts of the galaxy, presumably, hitting on this particular planet at the same time are greater than the odds against a monkey being able to pound out the U.N. Charter by randomly hitting typewriter keys."

"*We* got to Tantalus," Kwango pointed out.

Before Conrad could reply, there was a knock at the door.

"Come in."

It was Lieutenant Smith.

"I thought you were supervising the others," said Conrad somewhat coldly.

"I don't need to any more. It's late and I doped their drinks." She smiled. "They will have a very good night's sleep."

"I hope they won't be bloody sleepy in the morning."

"No problem. Pep shots in the coffee . . . Talking of drinks . . ."

"Help yourself," said Conrad.

Indira got her drink and sipped it gratefully. It was nice to be able to drink out of a glass once more instead of squeezing the fluid into your mouth from one of those dreadful bulbs.

"How is Pushkin?"

"Fit and well. I'll give him a thorough check-over tomorrow."

"Did he utter anything of interest?"

"He did. When he was just coming out of S.A. he said: 'Tell them I'll do it. Tell them I want to do it.' Then he passed out. Later, after I had given him basic orientation he asked: 'Who betrayed me?' I asked him what there was to betray. After that he laughed and said: 'Do you think I am entirely stupid.' Then he passed out again. I gave him a shot of adrenalin because his heartbeat was not so good. When he came back to consciousness, he was perfectly rational. He knew who he was, he knew who I was, and he knew why we were on Tantalus. He did not seem to be aware of his previous utterances. I judged it wise not to remind him . . . He has had his first meal—a huge one— and is now sleeping like a baby. He will be fit for light duties tomorrow and normal duty in a couple of days."

There was a brief silence, then Kwango said: "This

boy Alexei begins to sound interesting."

Conrad turned to Indira. "What is your opinion?"

She shrugged. "People say strange things when they come out of S.A. . . . It could relate to this situation, or it could relate to the murder of his wife, or some other situation we don't know about."

Conrad yawned. "I'll talk to him alone tomorrow. There are a lot of bloody things to do tomorrow. I'm going to get the chopper out and take a look at the rings. You, Kurt, will take the hover car and explore within a radius of ten kilometres, keeping your eyes open for Khelad's apelike creature. And you, Indira, will have the hardest task. I want you to stay here and keep an eye on the four. You can let them out two at a time, accompanied by robots. I think Zonis and Uhlmann should be the first out. Let them go and get more samples. If you want to keep Pushkin occupied, let him inspect the exo-skeletons. If you can spare a robot, Pushkin might begin assembling two or three. I have no doubt we shall need to use them pretty soon . . . Yes, tomorrow is going to be a very full day."

"What about Khelad?" asked Indira.

"Ah, yes, Khelad. Keep him monitoring the screen as long as seems reasonable. He is a very intriguing fellow, is our Ahmed. He is trying very hard to be liked."

"Do you think he really saw that creature?" asked Kwango.

"No way of knowing. Ahmed is a clever lad with a fine sense of timing."

Kwango finished his second drink. "Boss, you make a mistake. You told our new friends that the robots had been reprogrammed for homicide, if necessary. You know it can't be done, I know it can't be done. Pretty soon they are going to catch on."

"So they are," said Conrad tranquilly. "They were given the basic course in robotics before they joined us."

"Then why the hell did you make the statement?" said Indira. "The saboteur—if there is one—is going to think you are pretty damn stupid."

"Harsh words," said Conrad. He swirled his whiskey round in the glass and sniffed at it appreciatively. "If somebody wants to have a go at us, the robots will kill without hesitation. Matthew has override circuits. I have explained the situation to him. I have told him that, in a crisis situation, the life-function can be interrupted—just as, for example, it is interrupted in S.A. The robot concerned should strike at the heart and on no account must there be any brain damage. Matthew knows that we have bio-hearts and electro-mechanical hearts in store. I assured him that interruption of function would only be temporary . . . It is the old double-bluff with variation on a theme."

"I still don't like it," said Indira.

"Lieutenant, I did not ask you to like it," snapped Conrad. "Long ago, I learned that if you wish to survive, you fight fire with fire. Now let's all get some sleep."

HEADS YOU WIN, TAILS YOU LOSE

Conrad was up before daybreak. Automatically, he checked the security of the *Santa Maria*. John, Peter and Paul were at their guard posts in the sensitive areas. They had received no visitors. The night had passed without incident.

On the nav deck, Matthew stared impassively at the screens.

"Anything to report, Matthew?" It was a stupid question. The robot had his instructions. He would have called Conrad if there had been anything.

"Nothing of significance, sir. A number of small creatures resembling the terrestrial bat appeared at dusk and again just before daybreak. Their numbers were not at any time critical."

"Good. Have Peter bring me coffee and a bacon sandwich. I'll take it here."

"Decision noted, sir. Execution proceeds. Request precise definition of terms, also quantity required."

"Dammit, Matthew! You know how I take my coffee and bacon."

"Previous data has been variable, Commander. Of the two hundred and ninety-three times you required coffee on Kratos, on one hundred and seventy-three occasions you ordered—"

"Cancel statement," said Conrad wearily. "You are a

bloody ass—no, cancel that statement also . . . Definition follows: coffee, one half litre, hot, strong, black, sweet. Bacon, smoked, two twenty-five centimetre rashers grilled, crisp. Bread, slices, one, white. Definition adequate?"

"Definition adequate," said Matthew with just a hint of robotic humour. "Delivery time estimated at six point five minutes S.E.T. plus or minus three percent from now."

"I will take it over here," said Conrad. "I'll watch the screens while I am having my breakfast. I want the chopper and hovercar out of the hold and lowered dirtside. They will be used about two hours from now. During that time you and such of your merry band—Mark and Luke, I think—as are not on security duty will check engines, fuel, controls, every vital component. Execute!"

"Decisions noted, sir. Execution proceeds. Is the Commander aware that such inspections were carried out in Earth orbit and also in Tantalus orbit?"

"The Commander is aware," retorted Conrad, "and intends to stay that way. Call Lieutenant Smith to the nav deck at her earliest convenience. Do not designate emergency."

"Decision noted. Execution proceeds."

Somehow, Matthew contrived to leave the nav deck with heavy robotic dignity.

Lieutenant Smith arrived before the coffee and the bacon sandwich. She looked a little dishevelled and sleepy still. The white hair was straggly but strangely attractive. She had fine features, thought Conrad, as if seeing her again for the first time. He remembered those idyllic days at Applecross in the North West Highlands of Scotland. Her light brown skin was beautiful, and the fact that she had tin legs didn't matter a damn. He remembered that the real limbs had been cut off by a bunch of crazy South

American thugs who called themselves freedom fighters. They had cut her legs off after they had raped her and compelled her lover to watch. Then they had gouged his eyes out. Conrad hoped desperately that she did not have nightmares any more. He suspected she did. What had happened to her would be burned into her brain for ever.

His own prosthetic arm twitched, and he scratched his silver eye patch nervously. Damn! That was a stupid habit. He really must learn to control it.

"You sent for me, sir." Her voice was cold.

"I did, Lieutenant."

He took her in his arms and kissed her. At first she struggled. Then she stopped struggling. It wasn't possible to break the hold of a prosthetic arm.

"I could bring up my tin knee and knock your manhood into your throat," she gasped.

Conrad smiled and stroked her hair. "You could, but you won't." Her body had already told him. "This is the only way I know how of saying I'm sorry for being a bastard."

"James, you really are a bastard."

"Yes. I know. Forgive me. I do the best I can . . . Shall I enter in the log: This day Commander James Conrad improperly held his Second-in-Command without her consent?"

Indira kissed him and clung to him. "No. Write that Commander James Conrad. D.S.S.C. and bar, Grand Cross of Gagarin, briefly remembered Applecross."

Peter brought the coffee and the bacon sandwich. They heard him enter while they were enjoying the playback— and sprang apart guiltily. Then they looked at each other and laughed.

"One half litre of coffee and one bacon sandwich, as requested, Commander. Have the specifications been met?"

Conrad inspected the coffee and the bacon. He seemed almost disappointed that he could find no fault. "The specifications have been met." He turned to Indira. "Would you like some?"

"Bacon sandwich?" she shuddered. "James, you are a vandal."

"A bastard vandal," he corrected, grinning.

She turned to Peter. "Bring me a beaker with two centimetres depth of cream in it."

"Decision noted. Execution proceeds."

When the robot had gone, Conrad said: "Indira, my love, you had better go back to being Lieutenant Smith."

"Yes, sir." She smiled. "But it was nice to know that the good Commander has not erased his memory bank."

"I have been thinking about what I planned last night. It seems a lot to ask you to nurse our suspects while Kwango and I sally forth. Would you like to take the hovercar? Kurt can manage things here."

She shook her head. "Stop thinking of me as a woman. I'm your Number One. Kurt is better equipped for the survey. He knows what to look for and how to relate the evidence he finds. Don't worry. I have Matthew and company to back me up."

They were both watching the screens. And they both got a good look at the ape-like creature that Khelad had seen. Only this time there were several. At a pre-arranged signal, evidently, they rose up out of the grass and tossed small objects with their prehensile tails.

The muffled explosions shook the *Santa Maria*. Screen One went dead, screens Two, Three and Four went dead.

"Christ!" said Conrad. "They have knocked out the vid cameras!"

He hit the emergency button.

CRASH!

Accompanied by two robots and armed with a laser rifle, Kwango went dirtside as fast as he could. There was nothing to be seen except the small craters where the vid tripods had been. It looked as if chemical explosives had been used; but, strangely, the soil was steaming hot. He tested for radioactivity. There was some, but it was minimal.

He reported back by radio to the *Santa Maria*. "No sign of the little folk, Boss. It is rather warm where they took out the vids, but there is no radiac worth mentioning. No burn signs, either. Almost certainly, they used conventional explosives—unless their science is radically different from our science."

"Don't rule out the possibility," retorted Conrad drily. "Investigate thoroughly for a radius of one thousand metres and come back. If these people are smart—and I think they are—they will have got the hell out fast. By now, they are probably sitting somewhere about five kilometres away, waiting to see how we react."

"Can I take the hovercar and make a wider search?"

"No, you cannot. Now that we know for sure there is intelligence—hostile intelligence—on Tantalus, we minimise risks."

There was a brief silence. Then Kwango said: "How do you know they are people, Commander?"

"In my book," said Conrad, "people are intelligent creatures who know what they are doing and why they are doing it."

Kwango laughed. "That definition would include dolphins and robots."

"Exactly. Now do your sweep and get back. I don't think you will find anything, but make damn sure you test for the presence of metals as well as radioactivity."

"You think they may have left souvenirs?"

"If they wanted to get real tough, they might have put down a few proximity mines. Sweat on that. Over and out."

"Thanks, Boss. It's the thought that counts. Over and out."

Fortunately, there were no proximity mines—or none that went off. When he had covered the specified area, Kwango recalled the robots and returned to the *Santa Maria*.

Conrad held his conference in the saloon. "You have heard the descriptions—such as they are—of these creatures. So, at least, when you go dirtside you will know something about one of the dangers that you are likely to encounter. The fact that there are intelligent beings on Tantalus affects the nature of our mission. If these creatures have a sophisticated culture and are present in considerable numbers, it is highly likely that, even if we proved the planet to be fit for colonisation, U.N. would not sanction it."

"Then why don't we lift off and go home?" It was Alexei Pushkin speaking. He looked strong and healthy now, showing no signs of his recent trauma.

"Because nothing's yet proved," said Conrad patiently. "Orbital survey has yielded no evidence of cities, technology, energy consumption, radio emission—all the things you would associate with an advanced society. There's the mystery of the rings. But until we have solved it and until we know a great deal more about the creatures that took out the vids, we stay and explore."

"Commander," said Lisa Uhlmann, "may I suggest that you contact Terra, give the data already obtained, and await instructions?"

"No, you may not, Uhlmann," snapped Conrad. "It cost a lot to get us here. We do our work, we investigate the planet, and we don't lift off until we have all the answers."

Ahmed Khelad said: "I agree with Commander Conrad. We have a job to do. Let's do it."

Conrad became more irritable. "Strangely, Khelad, I don't need your agreement. I make my own decisions . . . Incidentally, I want you to design a rather special kind of mine. It has to be simple enough for the robots to be able to manufacture it in quantity. It has to be unaffected by temperature and moisture. It has to be triggered by a pressure of not less than twenty-five kilos, and it has to contain an explosive that will not do too much damage. What I want, basically, is a warning device—a deterrent not a destroyer. Can you do this?"

Khelad smiled. "But, of course."

"Good. There is, however, one small problem. For all I know, you may be our hypothetical saboteur, waiting for just such an opportunity. I know nothing about explosives, but Uhlmann is a chemist. Therefore she will supervise your work and you will explain every step to her. O.K.?"

The Arab shrugged. "I see the necessity, Commander, but I would have preferred to be trusted . . . It is not without the bounds of possibility that Uhlmann—no offence intended, Lisa—may be the saboteur, if there is one. Have you thought of that, Commander?"

"I have. I am gambling on the probability that you can't both be out to wreck this mission. She checks you, you check her and Lieutenant Smith checks the four of you. That is the way it has to be."

Conrad glanced at all of them. "Now, we are all going to have a busy day. I am going to take the chopper and have a look at the rings, Kwango will use the hovercar to survey the terrain within a radius of ten kilometres, the robots—such as can be spared—will construct an electrified defence perimeter. Zonis will go out and collect more bio-specimens, Pushkin will supervise the assembly of exo-skeletons and will use one to punch in the support girders for the defence system; and Lieutenant Smith, in my absence, will be in command. Any questions?"

Ruth Zonis said: "What happens if we are attacked while you are away?"

"Unless the safety of the *Santa Maria* is threatened, you will not retaliate. If the vessel itself is attacked, you will throw everything you have—at the discretion of Lieutenant Smith."

Conrad took the chopper up to an altitude of three hundred metres and circled slowly round the *Santa Maria*. Down below, three robots, looking like odd, metallic insects, were already at work on the defence perimeter. Sections of exo-skeleton were being lowered from the star-ship's derrick; and a small human figure—presumably Pushkin—waited dirtside to receive them. Kwango, in the hovercar, was already proceeding cautiously on his reconnaissance. So far, situation normal.

He called Lieutenant Smith. "Chopper to *Santa Maria*. Do you read me?"

"Loud and clear. How does it look from up there, James?"

"Very peaceful. Visibility good. I can just about see the ring system. I'm pushing off to take a closer look in a minute or two. Meanwhile, I'll just flip round and see if I can spot any of the jokers who took out our vids."

He brought the chopper down to one hundred and fifty metres and took it spirally out from the star-ship until he was more than a kilometre away.

He reported back. "As far as I can see, our destructive little friends are conspicuous only by their absence . . . Maybe Kurt will turn up something. Meanwhile, I'm lifting high and I am going to take a good look at the rings . . . Contingency plans. If I am not back in three hours, do not—repeat, do not—send out any search party. If I do not respond to radio signals confine all activity within perimeter defence. Kwango may use an exo-skeleton for a one-man search at your discretion. But if he does and he does not return you will abort this mission. Understood, Lieutenant?"

"Understood, Commander. Be careful and come back. It will save us all a lot of problems."

"I will. Over and out."

Conrad lifted to one thousand metres, then he headed slowly north. It was a fine, sunny morning. The country below looked good. Good and rich. Perfect for colonisation. Unless, of course, it held too many nasty surprises— which seemed quite unlikely.

Conrad thought yet again of the half-glimpsed creatures who had taken out the vids. They had known exactly what to do, and they had accomplished it with rapid efficiency. Then they had melted away. All the signs pointed to a high order of intelligence, which was fascinating on one level and depressing on another. Even if the Expendables could establish a bridgehead on Tantalus, U.N. was hardly likely to sanction a colonisation programme if it was known that the planet already supported a hostile and intelligent life-form. And yet, there remained the enigma of the planet's total technological "silence". No cities, no trace of civilisation, no sign of radio emission, industrial complexes, atomics—anything. Only the bloody great mystery of the rings and the equally great mystery of a huge, derelict star-ship.

Conrad's head ached. It ached, as he well knew, because his neural circuits were overloaded. He was having to worry about too many things—about a possible saboteur, about the nature of the rings, about the derelict star-ship and about creatures with prehensile tails who could lob bombs with deadly accuracy.

He tried to forget his headache and concentrate on his immediate task. The grassland was behind him. He was over the forest. He could see the ring system plainly. It was only about fifteen kilometres ahead.

He decided to move in very slowly and circle the system. It looked formidable. A vast area of the forest must have been cleared before the rings could be constructed.

The rings glistened in the morning sunlight. From this distance, they looked as if they might have been manufactured from copper or bronze. But telemetric investigation had shown that they were not metallic.

He lifted the chopper to three thousand metres, cancelled the forward thrust, hovered and looked down.

There was no sign of movement anywhere. He took a

pair of 30 × 50 binoculars and swept the area. As far as could be ascertained, it was completely free of animal life or bird life. As he had passed over the forest, he had seen a number of four-legged creatures—mostly small, but some strangely similar to the terrestrial deer or horse. And the passing of the chopper had disturbed two or three flocks of birds. But here, in the immediate vicinity of the ring system there was only desolation. Not even any plant life. The ground was bare, as if it had been sterilised.

For a moment or two, Conrad felt that he was looking down at some strange, alien cemetery. Human beings, in bygone ages when there was no shortage of land, had buried their dead in a great variety of ways. In the Stone Age, megaliths had been used as markers for clan chiefs; the Pharaohs had committed the extraordinary extravagance of pyramids; even in the twentieth and twenty-first centuries, when cremation and recycling were established procedures, many who could afford the luxury had chosen to have their remains interred in valuable ground and their small achievements commemorated by marble monuments.

Perhaps that was the case on Tantalus. Perhaps Conrad was looking down on the local equivalent of the pyramids. The most spectacular graveyard on the planet.

Suddenly, he experienced intense feelings of uneasiness, apprehension, fear. There was sweat on his forehead, and he did not know why.

He had the sense to report back to the *Santa Maria*. "Conrad speaking. I am over the ring system at three thousand metres. There are no signs of life. But I have begun to experience intense emotional disturbance. I can think of no rational explanation. It is my intention to circle the system, take pix and return. I think—"

The radio went dead. The green light, indicating normal transmission, just winked out. Conrad barely had time to register the fact before the chopper's atomic engine also died. Then the circuitry on the instrument panel folded.

The chopper began to lose altitude. Conrad had the wit to disengage the vanes from the engine so that they could rotate freely under air pressure. That way, he would not fall out of the sky like a stone. The landing would not be soft; but with a bit of luck it would be bearable. In any case, he could always hit the ejector-seat button and come down by parachute.

He glanced down at the rings. Was it his imagination, or were they becoming brighter, glowing almost? They were becoming brighter. Now they were almost luminescent.

He tried the radio again. No use.

The chopper was coming down fast. Too fast. It might survive impact and be salvageable. But flesh and bones were more vulnerable than titanium and steel. Conrad checked his harness, then braced himself and hit the button. He should have been blasted clear. He wasn't. Nothing happened. He hit the button again. Still nothing happened.

He looked once more at the rings. Goddammit, they were incandescent. The light hurt his eyes.

This is crazy, he thought. All my bloody power system knocked out, and those goddamn things are turning on like search-lights. He tried to swing the chopper into the wind —what there was of it—by manual controls. He partly succeeded, got her tail down a little and slowed the rate of fall. But the ground was still coming up far too fast. Thank God he wasn't over the forest!

It's going to be one hell of a bump, he told himself.

With a curious detachment, he tried to estimate his chances of survival. Two to one against, he thought. It seemed reasonable to be mildly pessimistic.

In the last few seconds before impact, he braced himself and tried to remember the orders he had given to cover just such a contingency. He couldn't remember a thing.

Then the crash came. He heard the fabric of the seat tear and felt a tremendous jarring. Then he was flung upwards and felt something smash into his bio-arm before the world of Tantalus knocked him on the head and brought a merciful oblivion.

The people who had designed the chopper had designed it well. They had used hiduminium and titanium and they had built into it three different systems of shock absorbers. They had planned for survival of the pilot if the motors failed.

The chopper hit and bounced. It hit and bounced again. Then it hit once more, listed and fell gently and just keeled over, its vanes crumpling as they bit into the ground. Conrad was already unconscious. He did not care a shit when the chopper came finally to rest.

A CALL TO ARMS

Conrad fought back to consciousness. As he came up to the lighter level, and before he could open his eyes, he was aware of the pain. The temptation to drift off once more and let it all go away was very great. He realised vaguely that he would not have too much difficulty slipping back into the darkness; but he determined to fight his way up to the light.

The pain got stronger. He tasted his own blood where he had bitten his tongue. Finally he opened his eyes. It took him some time to focus, but he managed it. Now he knew why he felt so much pain. His bio-arm was broken.

It looked bloody funny with a piece of the radius sticking through the skin of the smashed forearm. He couldn't see what had happened to the ulna. In any case, he didn't really want to know.

"Thank God it wasn't the prosthetic arm," he said aloud. Then he began to laugh. That was a fucking stupid remark to make. If the prosthetic arm had been smashed, he wouldn't have felt such pain.

Then he realised it wasn't such a stupid thing to say. The bio-arm could be repaired on Tantalus—if he lived. The prosthetic arm, a miracle of advanced engineering, could not. Big joke.

He had difficulty stopping the laughter. He knew all about hysteria. He had once seen a man with half his stomach blown away, laughing like crazy. But hysteria was difficult to control when it happened to be your own. He bit his tongue some more. That stopped him laughing. It also made him faint. When he came to again, he ordered himself to stop thinking about the broken arm, and took stock of his surroundings.

The chopper had come to rest at an angle of about forty-five degrees and he was hanging half-out of the pilot's doorway, held in position only by his safety harness. His bio-arm flopped over his chest, oozing blood, like carelessly butchered meat. He used his prosthetic arm to straighten it a little, then wished he hadn't. He blacked out.

Next time he came to, he knew what the optimum move would be. His prosthetic hand hit the harness release stud. He fell out of the chopper. He had expected to pass out yet again, but he didn't. He just lay on the ground, suffering and groaning for a while and feeling immensely sorry for himself.

Then he experienced shame. The shame was stronger than the pain. It gave way to anger. As adrenalin pumped through his system, he examined the damage—professionally. Apart from the arm, he was bruised all over and he hurt all over. When he breathed deeply there was a nasty little pain in his chest. Maybe a bust rib, maybe not.

But his legs were O.K. That was a great relief. He was going to have to use them. It would be a long walk back to the *Santa Maria*. Using his prosthetic arm to hold his bio-arm carefully in the position that gave least discomfort, he stood up.

Waves of blackness surged disturbingly over him, and there was a great roaring in his head. But miraculously, he did not fall. He swayed, but he did not fall. That, he told himself, was an important victory.

The chopper was a right mess—vanes curled like the petals of a withered flower; undercart smashed beyond belief; tail twisted up like a scorpion about to sting.

Idly, he wondered if Pushkin could fix it. Academic problem. The trick was to get back to the *Santa Maria*.

Carefully and slowly, he looked all around him. The chopper had hit the deck just over one kilometre from the nearest ring. It wasn't glowing any more. The fact was interesting. He tried to work out why, but he couldn't.

He had half expected a battalion of little green men—or, at least, monkeys with prehensile tails—to be rushing towards the wrecked chopper. But there was no living thing in sight.

It was a great relief.

Slowly, he got his wits back, recovered his bearings. He knew from the position of the sun which way he would have to go to get back to the *Santa Maria*. He tried to estimate how long it would take him in his present condition to walk twenty-five kilometres. With a bit of luck, he thought, he might make it before nightfall. *If* he didn't bleed too much, *if* he didn't pass out, if he could cope with the pain in his mangled arm, *if* some bloody carnivore didn't get the smell of blood and have a go, *if* he didn't start marching round in circles once he was in the forest.

"To many fucking ifs!" he said aloud. The sound of his own voice was, at least, some small comfort.

He looked down at his mangled arm—held firmly to his chest by his prosthetic arm—and wished he hadn't. The bleeding had almost stopped—which was something. But it looked one hell of a mess, all blotchy and blue and swollen and bloodstained. And there was the smashed radius. Only about three centimetres was now poking through the flesh; but it looked fairly horrible.

"Jesus!" he said. "The bloody bugs! The bugs of Tantalus!"

He wanted to sit down and scream. God alone knew what alien micro-organisms had already settled down to have a good time in the wound. He denied himself the luxury of sitting down and screaming. It would be—as they used to say—counter-productive.

Instead, he exercised his intelligence. In the chopper there was an emergency pack. Bandages, antiseptics, analgesics, splints, boosters, water, brandy, food concentrates.

"Look arm," he said in what he hoped was a reasonable tone, "you are going to have to hang loose for a few moments while Fred—that's my tin arm—finds something to keep you happy. Think you can make it?"

The broken arm did not protest. Conrad took that as a kind of assent.

He lurched back to the chopper's personnel bubble. Very carefully, he lowered the bust arm and let it hang loosely. Waves of pain came up and crashed against his mind. With a supreme effort he cancelled them.

He crawled back into the bubble and found the emergency pack. His prosthetic arm managed to snatch it out before his legs became rubber and he had to sit down.

In the pack there were various one-shot hypos, colour-coded. The red ones contained knock-out shots, the blue ones contained pain-killers, the green contained stimulants. He took a blue one and pressed the small plastic hemisphere resolutely into his arm. Then, while he waited for that to take effect, he started chewing dextrose tablets. He figured he was going to need a fair amount of sugar.

Presently, he felt better. The pain wasn't bothering him too much now. Deliberately, he bent his arm to open the wound as much as possible. Then he took a small can of aerosol antiseptic and squirted it all over. The stinging sensation was almost pleasant compared to the ebbing pain.

To calm himself down after that little effort, he took some brandy. He carefully measured the amount, knowing that in his present state he could get pissed very easily.

Then he straightened his arm and started to wind self-adhesive bandage round it. When he came to the break, he bound in a couple of light plastic splints. Finally, he slipped one of the adjustable slings over his head and nursed the smashed arm into it.

That accomplished, he felt better. Much better. He celebrated by taking one more small shot of brandy. Then he stuffed his pockets with food concentrates, slung a canteen of water round his neck and stood up.

He glanced around. Still no sign of little green men or even monkeys with hands on the ends of their tails. He was greatly relieved.

"March, Conrad," he said. "You are going to get back to the *Santa Maria* before nightfall. That is an order."

"Decision noted," he answered himself, trying unsuccessfully to mimic Matthew's metallic voice. "Execution proceeds."

Conrad marched. Or, more accurately, staggered towards the green wall of the forest.

Phase Seven

ENTER THE U.S. CAVALRY

As he went into the forest, Conrad got the sudden impression that he was being watched. He stopped, glanced all around him and could see nothing. He pressed on, trying to shake off the feeling, telling himself that he was in a highly nervous condition. But the sensation persisted. He began to sweat profusely, though the forest was not unpleasantly warm.

"Dammit, I have a right to be shit scared," he said aloud. "I've fallen out of the sky, bust my arm, and I have to make it on foot back to the ship. I don't know a thing about this lousy world . . . Don't even know whether or not there are any dangerous animals or whether the whole shebang is as safe as Kew Gardens on a wet Sunday. No wonder I'm sweating. Probably some tiny little bug I can't even see will bite me in the arm and give me a one-way ticket. It was an amusing thought. He began to laugh. Then he realised that he was going to pieces.

"Stop that, Conrad!" he snapped. "You are guilty of negligence and dereliction of duty. You lost the chopper and you didn't even bring a laser rifle. You deserve to be court-martialled. Now get the hell back, and stop whining."

It worked—for a while. Resolutely, he marched forward. But the green umbrella of the forest was hypnotic, and the sense of being watched persisted.

He tried an experiment. He ran fifty paces as fast as he

could, trying to ignore the pain that was coming back to his broken arm. Then he stood still and listened. Was it imagination or were there other bodies crashing through the undergrowth? He could not be sure. The noise stopped almost as soon as he stopped.

He sat down, got his breath, waited for the throbbing in his arm to subside, swallowed some more dextrose. Then he got up and walked.

Presently, he was amazed to find that he had fallen down. He had not tripped over anything. He had just fallen down. He looked at the bandage on his arm. It was bright red—red and wet and dripping. He was still aware of the sensation of being watched, but it did not seem to matter any more.

"Law of diminishing returns," he muttered thickly and incomprehensibly. He drank some water, then stood up, swaying.

When the roaring in his ears had stopped, when the mists had cleared, he marched forward again. It seemed a good idea to count his paces. Something to do. He counted.

He made two hundred and forty-seven paces before he fell down again. He was tired. He wanted to sleep.

"Conrad," he said, "you are a stupid bastard. Get on your feet, man! March, you stupid specimen, march! And count your fucking steps."

He managed two hundred and twenty-three steps before he fell down again.

More dextrose, more water. He stopped sweating. He began to shiver.

"Get up, swine!" he grated. "Call yourself a man, you chicken-hearted zombie! Get up and march."

Conrad did not recognise the voice, but he did not like

the tone. It was offensive. Not nice. Definitely nasty.

"Piss off, whoever you are. I'll do it my way."

Nevertheless, Conrad stood up and staggered forwards, counting.

One hundred and nineteen paces, and he hit the dirt. With a supreme effort of will he got up again and went on. Seventy-three paces—or was it sixty-three?—and he hit the dirt once more.

He didn't feel like getting up again. He tried it twice and failed. The third time he was cunning. He told himself he was just playing a game, conned himself into crouching, then stretched suddenly. He went out like a light.

Next thing he knew, there was a great metal monster standing over him. A giant. A fantastic creature, vaguely humanoid in form. A colossus.

"What the hell are you?" he asked faintly.

He felt he ought to know the voice that answered. It was vaguely familiar, but he was just too tired to identify it.

"Boss, I am the resurrection and the life. Take it easy. You have had a hard day."

Then great metal hands came down and scooped Conrad up as if he were a baby.

"Rest easy, Boss," said the strangely familiar voice. "You've had a rough time. Don't worry yourself no more. Bang on schedule, de U.S. cavalry has come over de hill."

Kwango!

Conrad was immensely pleased that he had finally identified the voice. Kwango in an exo-skeleton.

Commander James Conrad uttered a great sigh and went peacefully to sleep.

Stage Three

SHOWDOWN

Phase One

THE IMPORTANT PATIENT

The first thing Conrad saw when he opened his eyes was the face of Lieutenant Smith. Her white hair was a bit disordered, but she looked beautiful. He had a feeling of *déja vu*.

"Good morning, James. I hope you had a good sleep. I have filled you full of anti-biotics and set the arm properly. I had to do a bit of fancy needlework also, but it will hardly show. You were in quite a state."

"How did Kwango find me?"

She shrugged. "You know Kurt. The Gods gave him too many talents—fortunately for us. He worked out some kind of search pattern based on your probably flight-path, harnessed himself in the exo and departed at thirty knots. You have seen what he can do in an exo-skeleton. Be thankful."

"I am."

"Now for the bad news. I have assumed temporary command of the *Santa Maria*. It is entered in the log and countersigned by Kwango. All legal. I shall retain command until, in my judgment, you are a fit person. Understood, Commander?"

Bloody woman! Now he knew it really was *déja vu*. It had happened on Kratos also. Only there he had smashed himself up having a go at the death worms.

"Understood, Commander?" she repeated with an edge of hardness in her voice.

He sighed. "Understood—Commander." His head was clear and he felt fit enough to get up and resume duty. But what the hell use was that if she was backed up by Kwango? She would only get Kurt to hold him down while she shot a needleful of sleep-juice into him. She was that kind of woman. "How long is the sentence this time?"

Indira smiled. "Three days if you are lucky."

"Do I get any remission for good behaviour?"

"I'll think about it. Meanwhile, do you feel fit enough to explain how you, an experienced pilot, managed to smash the chopper?"

"I do."

At that moment Kwango came into the cabin. "So the good Commander is alive and well . . . Boss, you have been a very naughty boy. If you don't behave yourself, the Lieutenant and I are not going to let you play with any more expensive toys for quite a while. And how do you like that?"

"I don't. Thanks for picking me up, Kurt, but spare me the funnies."

"How came you to bust the chopper—drunken driving?"

"Kurt, my prosthetic arm is still O.K. Remember that."

Kwango laughed. "Right, Commander. Now tell it like it was."

Conrad remembered vividly all that had happened. He recounted the sequence of events concisely, accurately.

When he had finished, Kwango let out a low whistle. "So the rings can knock out atomic engines, control systems, radio communications."

"So it would appear. We haven't discovered much about

Tantalus so far; but what we have discovered is rather unnerving . . . How long have I been out, by the way?"

"About thirty hours," said Indira. "I could have let you rejoin us sooner, but I thought you needed the rest. I had to put quite a lot of plasma into you. I hope you have an appetite because you are shortly going to eat a meal of lightly cooked liver, washed down with half a litre of red wine."

Conrad rolled his eyes and grinned. "Oh, the terrors of the sick bay!"

Kwango said: "Returning to the problems of Tantalus, there is something else you are not going to like too much, Boss. While you were off playing strange games with the rings, I went on my proximity survey and bagged one of those interesting little critters with prehensile tails."

"You killed it?"

"In a manner of speaking."

Conrad tried to sit up, and wished he hadn't. Waves of pain ran up his bio-arm and made his head throb. His vision blurred and he almost passed out.

Lieutenant Smith noted his reaction. "Serve you right," she said. "You don't do anything—I mean anything—without my say so. You will now rest until the meal is prepared."

With an effort, Conrad managed to control his temper. "Permission to continue my discussion with Kwango?" he asked meekly.

"Five minutes only." She went towards the door. "When I come back, you eat the liver—all of it—and rest. Understood?"

"Damn you, yes!" Conrad wanted to hit her.

Lieutenant Smith turned. "May I remind you," she said softly, "that you are speaking to the temporary commander of this expedition. Your behavior and reactions as a patient will undoubtedly affect my judgment of the time when you are fit to resume normal duties."

Conrad turned red. He was about to make some malicious reference to Applecross, then thought better of it. "Yes, sir. I apologise, Commander." He cleared his throat and spit out the words like plum stones. "No offence intended."

"Keep it that way, spaceman," she retorted. "Until I decide otherwise you are just an injured man in a bed."

She left before he could explode. Conrad turned his frustrated anger on Kwango.

"You are not empowered to destroy intelligent indigenes. Explain yourself, black man!"

"Cool it, Boss. You get yourself all worked up, and de good Lieutenant—I mean temporary Commander—is going to keep you here longer than you think."

"O.K. I get the message. Now, what happened?"

"I was cruising along in the hovercar—actually, I was following a herd of quadrupeds that look like zebras and might be a potential meat supply—when this joker rose up out of the grass about a hundred metres ahead of me. It looked as if it was about to toss something playfully— like the grenades that took out the vids. So I lasered it." Kwango shrugged. "I only had the laser on minimum power. Didn't want to do too much damage, thinking that Zonis might want to take a look at what was left. But, Boss, that creature fell flat on its tiny, and then went up boom. Seems it had a grenade or some such, after all. The pieces were still raining down when I got to the crater."

"Hm . . . Did you collect any of the bits?"

"Yes, Commander. Here comes the part you are not

going to like too much. It wasn't an animal. It was a robot."

Conrad forgot himself, tried to sit up again, again wished he hadn't. He waited patiently for the pain to subside. Then he said weakly: "Goddammit!"

Kwango permitted himself a cautious smile. "My sentiments exactly, Commander. The circuitry, the technology and the hardware—judging from the pieces I found—are so far ahead of our science as to make me feel like a Stone Age savage . . . Matthew is the most advanced kind of robot we have. He is built like a tank, weighs about two hundred kilos, and looks like an antique washing machine on legs. The robot I lasered was light, compact, extremely agile. Also it had a bio-skin. The innards were electronic and mechanical. But the skin was a living organism."

"Who says so?"

"Zonis says so. She is still doing her nut trying to figure out how it could work."

"Have you got any more bad news?"

"Yes, if you don't already have enough. The Khelad-Zonis thing is blowing up again. Zonis loses no opportunity to taunt Khelad whenever she can. She seems determined to make him lose his cool."

"It could still be an elaborate act," said Conrad, "designed to put us off the scent."

Kwango shrugged. "I don't think so. I think Ruth is playing it for real because she really believes Ahmed is the bad boy."

Conrad was silent for a moment or two. Then he said: "You like her a lot, don't you, Kurt?"

Kwango looked pained. "Boss, and with great respect for your prosthetic arm—which, as we both know, is temporarily useless because you can't even sit up—it's none of your damn business." Slowly, a grin spread across the black man's face. "And how the hell do you know?"

"I have noted the way you look at her, stupid. I mention this only because I am thinking of making an experiment which may possibly help to reduce our number of suspects. I am thinking of pairing her with Khelad as an exploratory team working without supervision. If, as I suspect, Zonis is—"

"Don't suspect, don't even think, and especially don't try to make decisions," said Lieutenant Smith, who had just returned to the sick bay, followed by Matthew, bearing the prescribed food and drink. "Your immediate mission is simply to recover from injuries sustained. Meanwhile, I do all the thinking and deciding. Incidentally, your five minutes is now up . . . Kurt, please carry out a check. Uhlmann and Zonis are in the lab, Khelad and Pushkin are dirtside within range of the screens."

"Will do, Commander."

As Kwango left, Conrad called: "How is Pushkin behaving? What do you think of him?"

Kwango half turned. "Very efficiently. Stout fellow. He plays a mean game of chess."

"Who won?"

Kwango smiled. "Oh, ye of little faith . . . He resigned on the thirty-first move."

Lieutenant Smith pressed a button, and Conrad was raised automatically to a sitting position.

"Now, eat," said Indira. "And eat it all if you don't want trouble."

Conrad said: "I don't want trouble."

He thought of Applecross and swore silently to himself that there would be a return match.

Phase Two

KWANGO'S TANGO

Lieutenant Smith allowed Conrad to resume full command only after six full days. On the morning of the third day he had developed a temperature nearly 2°C above normal. He rapidly lapsed into delirium and high fever. Lieutenant Smith shot him full of anti-biotics and then linked his circulatory system veinously to an oxygenator temperature control rig. She gave a mild oxygen boost and experimentally brought the temperature down ½°C. He coughed a little but seemed easier. That was the trouble with the O/T rig. You could oxygenate the blood and control temperature easily; but if you were not careful you wound up with respiratory problems and a cure that could be worse than the disease.

Matthew was thoroughly familiar with O/T procedure and could have handled the operation efficiently, but Lieutenant Smith preferred to do it herself. Despite having already done a heavy stint of duty, she stayed up all night with Conrad, constantly making small adjustments to the rig as his responses varied. Shortly before daybreak, she checked his heart and respiration for the nth time. Apart from a small and acceptable amount of fluid slopping around in the bronchia, all was well. She disconnected the O/T rig with a sigh of relief. Conrad could now go it alone.

Kwango came to relieve her. Red-eyed, she waved him away.

"You ought to get some sleep, Indira. Matthew can operate de white man's magic, and I can mind de store."

She smiled faintly and gestured towards the now peacefully sleeping Conrad. "Better not let that male chauvinist monster hear you calling me Indira. He doesn't know it—and he wouldn't admit it if he did—but he is a very possessive bastard."

"Yes, Ma'am, Commander, Sir," retorted Kwango solemnly. "My trouble is that I love you but I also love him—even though he is a one-armed shit."

Conrad opened his eyes, tried to focus, failed, and closed them again. "I heard that," he said weakly. "Kwango, for insolence and insubordination you are fined—"

"'One booze ration!" said Kwango and Lieutenant Smith simultaneously. Commander James Conrad gave a faint laugh and went back to sleep.

"Kurt, when did you last get some sleep?" asked Lieutenant Smith, noting that the black man was swaying slightly.

"I just came from my bed," he lied.

"Get back to it, then. That is an order. I know what you have been doing. You have been seeing to the safety of the vessel, the perimeter defence system, and the surveillance of our suspect colleagues. Sign off, Kurt. The robots can handle it."

"I am better than the robots."

"In most ways, yes. But the robots don't need to sleep: you do."

Kwango yawned. "Message received."

"Over and out."

Conrad discovered that a great deal had been accomplished during his time in the sick bay. The defence perimeter had been strengthened and behind that a solid stockade of outward-pointing sharpened tree trunks had been built. In that, Conrad detected the hidden hand of Kwango. He had helped build a similar stockade on Kratos as a protection against the death worms. Using an exo-skeleton, and looking like an armoured giant eight metres high, he had plucked up trees as if they were daisies, stripped and sharpened them and had tossed them neatly into pre-dug holes like darts.

Using an exo-skeleton was simply one of Kwango's many natural skills. Once in harness, he could make the anthropomorphic metal monster do the work of fifty men or ten robots. All of which gave Conrad an idea.

The chopper was wrecked, twenty-five kilometres away. But it was a useful, if not vital, piece of equipment. Maybe Kwango and Pushkin could mount a salvage operation . . .

As Conrad strolled about the compound, observing much industrious activity, he mulled over the data that had already been obtained. Biologically, Tantalus was an almost perfect planet for colonisation. But for the rings and but for the monkey-like robots. The first question was: where the hell were the intelligent indigenes, if any? The second question was: who, if anyone, was going to try to blow the project? Answers would have to be found pretty quickly. Otherwise, the proving project was doomed.

Alexei Pushkin came towards him. He had been making small adjustments to the control system in one of the exo-skeletons that lay on its back, reminding Conrad of metallic Martian creatures he had once read about as a boy. He tried to remember the title of the book, an early twentieth century novel which had great period charm. He could only remember the name of the author: John Wyndham.

"Glad to see you up and around Comrade Commander." The sturdy Russian seemed genuinely pleased that Conrad was fit for duty once more.

"Good morning, Alexei. You and I have not seen much of each other yet, I am afraid. No hard feelings for keeping you on ice longer than the others?"

Pushkin shrugged. "It doesn't matter. *I* know I'm not your saboteur; but I damn well bet I know who is, Comrade Commander."

"Who?"

The Russian smiled. "I prefer not to say."

"Do you have any evidence?"

"No. I have only the intuition. That is why I do not wish to give the name. But I am watching this person very closely, I can tell you."

"I could order you to give me the name."

"You could—and I could lie to you. You would have no means of knowing I spoke the truth. So is not very good deal, *n'est ce pas, tovarish*?"

Conrad changed the subject. "You know how I wrecked the chopper, Alexei?"

"Yes. Kwango told me."

"We need that chopper. It is somewhat bent and busted. But I was wondering if—"

Pushkin beamed. "Say no more, Comrade Commander. I am, as you know, an engineer of some talent. There was no fire, I understand?"

"No, there was no fire. But there was a great deal of impact damage."

"It can be fixed. May I suggest that Comrade Kwango

and I use exo-skeletons to bring back the chopper for repair?"

Conrad nodded. He took his transceiver out of his pocket. "Kurt, where are you and what are you doing?"

After a moment or two, Kwango's voice came back. "With the computer, Boss. I've been going over the evaluation print-out. Also I have been doing some private thinking."

"What about?"

"The ring system. Boss, I think it could be some kind of fortress, or maybe a cosmic way-station."

"An interesting thought. Can you leave your speculation to return to matters practical?"

"What do you have in mind, Commander?"

"I want my chopper back and operational. Alexei says he can fix it. He says if you and he took a couple of exos—"

"What if the rings knock out the power systems, like they did to the chopper?"

"I was about to advise," snapped Conrad testily, "that one exo proceeds a kilometer ahead of the other. If it falls flat we will, of course, have lost another expensive item of equipment. But we will have learned something. I am prepared to gamble with an exo if there is a chance of getting the chopper back."

"I'll be right down," said Kwango. "If all goes well, am I empowered to take a close look at the rings while I am in the vicinity?"

"No, you are not. This is a salvage operation. I do not want to risk complications."

Lieutenant Smith came to watch the two men harnessing themselves into the exo-skeletons. The anthropomorphic machines were formidable things, atomically powered. They were eight metres long from feet to control crown. With a skilled operator in the control harness, the exo would amplify his strength by a factor of fifty. It would allow him to leap ten metres into the air or run across the countryside at seventy k.p.h.

Kwango was the first to harness up. He made his own exo stand, then he stretched out his massive steel arms, picked Pushkin's up and set it on its feet while the startled Russian was still checking his control web.

Conrad heard their interchange on his transceiver.

"Comrade! Easy, by damn! You will break my arm before we start."

Kwango laughed. "Broken arms are fashionable around here. That's the way to get tender, lovin' care from the good Lieutenant." He waved gaily down to the now pygmy-like forms of Conrad and Lieutenant Smith about twenty metres away, knowing that they had probably heard what he had said. "Ready now, Alexei?"

"Yes, I am ready."

"Good. I'll lead until we are about five kilometres from the rings. Then you take over. If any clockwork monkeys start tossing grenades, don't stay to play with them. The Commander gets cross if his toys are broken."

Suddenly, Kwango broke into a run, causing the ground to shake. He gave a tremendous leap, rose six metres into the air and cleared the entire defence perimeter. Pushkin marched sedately out through the double gateway.

"Kurt is full of *joie de vivre*," said Indira.

Conrad kept his fingers on the transmit stud of his transceiver. "He will also be full of grievous bodily harm, if he damages that exo."

"I heard that, Commander," came Kwango's voice.

"I know you did, you black bastard. Don't play clever or you'll wake up and find yourself in the intensive care unit. Over and out."

While Conrad was in the sick bay, a large workshop, the walls and room of which were made of local timber, had been erected as far from the *Santa Maria* as possible, close to the stockade gateway.

It was here that Conrad found Ahmed Khelad, Lisa Uhlmann and two robots. They had set up an assembly line for the production of the land mines that Conrad had ordered.

"Well, Ahmed, how goes the good work?"

Khelad gestured towards rows of metal objects, each shaped like a discus, that a robot was packing carefully into wooden boxes. "Your requirements have been met, Commander. The mines can only be triggered by a pressure of more than twenty-five kilos. The explosive agent is tri-nitro-cellulose, the ingredients of which have been obtained locally. The casing is of sheet duralumin, which fragments easily and will not do a great deal of damage."

"You have been working hard. How many do you have now?"

"About a hundred and eighty."

"I think we ought to have five hundred. Can you manage that?"

Khelad shrugged. "The tri-nitro-cellulose is no problem; but it will greatly reduce our supply of duralumin sheeting."

"Let us hope we can eventually make that good from local resources also. I believe Kwango has already established the presence of reasonably rich bauxite deposits."

He turned to Lisa Uhlman. "Has Ahmed been a good boy, Lisa?"

She tossed back her hair and laughed. Lisa Uhlmann had a very good figure, Conrad noted. He was surprised he had not noticed it before. Maybe it was because she had not wanted him to.

"Ahmed has been a model of Arab propriety, Commander."

"That wasn't what I meant."

"I know it wasn't. Don't worry. I can account for every gramme of explosive that has been produced."

"I am glad to hear it."

Khelad said: "Lisa is scrupulously honest and very efficient, Commander. It is a pleasure to work with her . . . Evenutally, you are going to realise that I am not your saboteur."

Conrad smiled. "Let us hope there is no saboteur. It looks as if Tantalus itself will provide all the sabotage we can handle."

Ruth Zonis was in the lab, peering down a microscope. She was examining tissue taken from a Tantalus "rabbit."

"What is the verdict?" asked Conrad.

Zonis stood up and stretched her arms back to ease the ache of concentration. Her breasts jutted out. Jesus, thought Conrad, I am too busy watching women today. I must do something about it.

"Commander, this is a viviparous creature rich in protein and trace elements. It has no fat and—as far as I can determine—no genetic abnormalities. It has a gestation of forty-seven days and produces a litter of between four and nine. Maturation takes about sixty days. The meat, when cooked, is white, soft and succulent. In food terms, as far as colonists are concerned, it is a goldmine. And how do you like that?"

"I like it very much," said Conrad.

"How is your arm?"

He glanced down at the sling. "Still stiff and fairly useless. I'm getting therapy. Lieutenant Smith takes sadistic pleasure in giving the muscles electric shocks."

Zonis laughed. "Lieutenant Smith is one hell of a woman. She didn't get much sleep while you were *hors de combat*."

"Yes . . . That would have been as good a time as any for a saboteur to strike."

"My thought also, Commander. I kept Ahmed in view as much as possible."

"Also, so I understand, you spent much time provoking him."

Ruth Zonis met Conrad's gaze. "I don't think I have committed any chargeable offence, Commander."

"No. But it is our duty to do our best to work harmoniously, otherwise this mission may fall flat without any sabotage. That is why I have special plans for you and Khelad."

Kwango and Pushkin returned shortly before dusk with the chopper. They carried it between them, each gripping one of the skids with an exo-arm, as if the machine were a toy. The vanes had been straightened and the machine looked to be in perfect condition.

They put the chopper down carefully, close to the *Santa Maria's* landing torus. Then they lay down in their exoskeletons and unharnessed. They had a story to tell. Pushkin began to tell it—succinctly.

"Comrade Commander, we followed the route you described. We found the helicopter without any difficulty. The marks of your crash had been eliminated, and the machine had been fully repaired."

"I wish you wouldn't call me Comrade Commander," snapped Conrad irritably, scratching his silver patch. "I'm not a bloody Communist, Pushkin." He suddenly realised he was scratching the patch, cursed silently and stopped it. Every bloody thing was getting out of hand.

"No, Comrade Commander. But I am." Pushkin grinned. "Also it is logical. You are my comrade as well as my commander . . . There is more. Do you wish to hear it?"

"Of course I bloody wish to hear it!"

"I think—that is, Kwango and I think—the helicopter was meant to be a trap. There were no signs of the monkey robots when we arrived. They must have been aware of our coming, because one cannot conceal one's existence in an exo-skeleton. But the moment Kwango and I lifted the machine, they came at us from all directions. They had weapons, but they were not permitted to use them." He laughed. "Kwango reacts very quickly in a time of crisis. He is a good man to have with you, that one."

"What happened then?" demanded Conrad testily.

Kwango took up the tale. "Sorry, Boss," he said apologetically, "I goofed. Instant reaction, and all that crap. As soon as I saw the critters, I told Alexei to put the chopper down." He grinned. "The clockwork monkeys weren't expecting exos. They were expecting people, such as they had already registered in their circuitry. They got a bad surprise. One of them tossed a grenade. I stooped, caught it and tossed it back. That took care of three of them. Then the rest joined in the fun. With grenades coming from all quarters, it seemed advisable for

Alexei and me to start jumping—which we did . . . Those robots weren't programmed to deal with agile, metallic giants. It was just like firecrackers going off round our feet . . . Anyway, I got mad and started stamping on them. I flattened about seven before the three or four survivors got the message. Sorry about that."

"So you should be," said Conrad coldly. "I was hoping not to start a bloody war."

"You said you wanted the chopper back."

"I did. But not at any cost."

"Boss, a state of war existed the moment they took out the vids. Also, knocking you out of the sky was hardly a big hello. If I hadn't flattened those robots, the chopper might have been damaged again or one or both of the exos might have been taken out. Then we would have been in real trouble."

"Maybe. At least, you're both back and the chopper is back. Which is something."

Phase Three

CONRAD GETS TOUGH

That evening after dinner, Conrad said: "It is time we took stock of ourselves and the situation we are in. We have not found the saboteur, if there is one; we have not established any contact with intelligent indigenes, if there are any; we have discovered robots who don't like us very much and will doubtless like us even less after Mr. Kwango's recent display of *joie de vivre*."

He looked at the six other Expendables seated at the saloon table. Lieutenant Smith returned his gaze and smiled faintly. Kwango seemed embarrassed, but probably was not. Pushkin, who had eaten a very large meal, looked rather contented, rather sleepy. Uhlmann and Khelad, sitting next to each other, seemed curiously intimate. Conrad suspected that Khelad's hand rested discreetly on her leg. Ruth Zonis, though flanked by Kwango and Indira, seemed strangely alone, mildly resentful.

"According to all the biological and geological evidence, Tantalus is ideal for colonisation, so we are going to go for broke. If any saboteur wishes to have a crack, he or she will have to do so in the next ten days. After that, there will be no opportunity."

"How's that again, Boss?" asked Kwango.

"Work it out for yourself, black man," snapped Conrad. "You are supposed to be the one with the big computer between his ears."

"I know what he means, Kurt," said Runth Zonis. "If goings go the way he wants, the Commander will put the four of us back in the cooler."

"Give the lady a cigar," said Conrad tranquilly. "It was the obvious solution. We can't spend an entire planetary cycle proving this planet, watching each other, and wondering all the time if somebody is going to pull the plug. So we go for broke. In the next ten days we are going to make a detailed survey of the land, flora and fauna within a radius of one hundred kilometres. We are going to make seismic surveys, magnetometric surveys and so on. We are also going to enter the ring system—blasting our way in, if necessary—to find out what it's all about. If we don't get knocked out by a saboteur, or by those monkey robots or by as yet undiscovered indigenes, four of you can sleep it off while Kwango, Lieutenant Smith and I complete the planetary survey and prove that human beings can survive a year of Tantalus."

"This is monstrous!" exploded Pushkin.

"No. Merely logical, comrade engineer," retorted Conrad drily. "With the help of the robots, the three of us can manage ten days at maximum alert."

"Commander, has it occurred to you that you may be paranoid?" asked Lisa Uhlmann softly.

Conrad laughed. "You must have studied the record of my court-martial on Luna . . . Yes, I may be paranoid, Lisa. It doesn't matter. I led the team that proved Kratos and gave another world to mankind. Tantalus looks as if it will be even better than Kratos. I don't care what the hell I do so long as we lick this planet and get the colonists rolling through the matter transmitter. If that is paranoia, I am content."

Khelad said: "Commander, may we assume that, if the saboteur is found, the rest of us will not be put in S.A.?"

"You may, Ahmed. Thus the goodly have a strong incentive to help. I am gambling, of course, that there is only one. It is now an acceptable risk. Incidentally, Ahmed, I understand that relations between you and Ruth are still not too good. You will have an opportunity to improve them. Until further notice, you and she will work as a team."

Ruth Zonis stood up. "I will not do it!" she flared. "If anyone is a saboteur, it is that man. I will not work with him."

"Zonis, you will obey orders," said Conrad evenly. "If you do not, you will immediately be placed in suspended animation. When we return to Earth, you will stand trial for mutiny. You will also complete your previous sentence for crimes committed against the state of Egypt."

Ruth Zonis put her hands to her face and made as if to leave the saloon.

"Sit down!" snapped Conrad. "You have not been dismissed."

She hesitated for a moment to two. Then, obediently, she returned to her chair and sat down.

"For the next few days, Pushkin will work with Kwango and Uhlmann will work with Lieutenant Smith. Get a good night's sleep, everyone. We are all going to be damn busy. Tomorrow, Khelad and Zonis will get on with production of the mines. When they have got the required five hundred, they will lay a random minefield outside the defence perimeter. They will, of course, leave an avenue free at the gateway and they will mark the exact position of each

mine on a large scale map. How long do you estimate it
will take, Ahmed?"

The Arab shrugged. "Three, perhaps four days. It is
difficult to tell." He gave a faint smile. "Much depends on
how co-operative Ruth will be."

"She will be very co-operative," Conrad assured him.
"Also she will be watching your every move—as, doubtless, you will be watching hers . . . How long?"

"Three days, then, Commander."

"Right. See that it is three days. Lieutenant Smith, you
and Uhlmann will make a survey to the south, using the
hovercar. You will construct maps, record the abundance,
characteristics and movements of all animal life and any
other data that is relevant to colonization. Kwango, you
and Pushkin will use exos and reconnoitre to the north.
You will map the terrain, record the behaviour of animal
life, etc. If you encounter robots or intelligent indigenes,
you will avoid provocation. If you are attacked, however,
and cannot withdraw, you will inflict only sufficient
casualties to discourage your attackers. At your discretion,
Kwango, you will approach the ring system as closely as
possible, endeavouring to determine its nature, its defence
capabilities and whether or not it can be entered with
or without use of force . . . Is anyone not clear about
his or her duties?"

There was silence.

"Well, then," said Conrad tranquilly, "let's all hit the
sack. It is going to be a hard ten days' night—for all of
us."

Later, Indira came to his cabin.

"You played it very rough, James."

"Intentionally. I don't like waiting for things to happen.

The saboteur—if we have one—now knows how much time there is left in which to operate. That ought to pile on the pressure."

"You are sure that is what you want?"

"Yes. I'm damn sure. One way or another, we will find out what the ring system is during the next ten days. Once we lick that, the rest should be relatively easy. If we haven't found the bad apple, we cool the four of them. Then you, Kwango and I can extend the survey at our leisure . . . My god, I'm tired."

"You have been doing too much, thinking too much. How does the arm feel?"

"It throbs and it itches."

"As your doctor, ideally I should prescribe two weeks of rest followed by four weeks of light duty."

Conrad grinned. "As your superior officer, I order you to get undressed and get into bed."

"You can't do anything with that arm as it is."

"Find out!" He took off the sling and threw it away.

"James, you are being unreasonable and illogical."

"I know. Get into bed."

"You are forgetting the house rules. On Kratos we—"

"Damn the house rules! What we did on Kratos doesn't apply here. The four new ones have yet to prove themselves as Expendables. But if you want to call Kurt and ask his permission . . ."

"I don't want to call Kurt," she said weakly. "You are a strange man, James Conrad, and I love you."

"Then get the hell into bed."

Conrad succeeded in making love—after a fashion— then fainted. Professionally, Indira checked pulses, temperature, respiration. He was O.K. Just exhausted. She held him close, laid his head on her breast, and listened to incoherent mumblings that went on almost through the night.

SUDDEN DEATH

In the morning, before Conrad went down to the saloon for breakfast, Indira got her medikit and pumped a stimulant into him. Conrad protested feebly.

"Last night you tried to play the big he-man," she said tartly, "and now you are paying the price. It is my turn to get tough. If you don't obey my instructions, I'll resume command—Kwango will back me up."

"O.K., Lieutenant." He gave a weak smile. "I like you better with your legs wide open."

"I should have known better," she retorted. "And I'll not open them again until you get sensible . . . Now, you will rest for half an hour while the rocket fuel goes through your system. I'll get one of the robots not on guard duty to bring you some coffee."

By the time he entered the saloon, the rest of the Expendables were finishing their breakfasts.

"You all know your tasks," he said crisply. "Get cracking as soon as you are ready. Check your transceivers before you push off. Matthew will be on duty at the communications console. Lieutenant Smith, you and Uhlmann will report back every hour on the hour. Kwango, you and Pushkin will report back every hour on the quarter past, Khelad, you and Zonis will report back every hour on the half past. Both the exploratory teams will be tracked by d/f. If either team fails to make its appointed signal, a search and rescue operation will be mounted. Good hunting."

Kwango grinned. "And what are you going to do, Commander?"

"I am going to sit at the centre of my spider's web and wait for flies."

Less than three quarters of an hour later, Khelad signalled from the shed where the mines were being assembled. Conrad was taking a leisurely bath. Since the signal was not a routine check-in. Matthew hooked Khelad's transmission to Conrad's bathroom 'phone.

"Commander, six of my mines are missing."

"I am not entirely surprised, Ahmed. Whom do you suspect?"

"Zonis, of course. But she has not been here very long, and I have watched her carefully. It is most puzzling."

"Well. The mines are theoretically, non-lethal, aren't they?"

"Yes. But if six are linked together and detonated simultaneously . . ."

"I take your point. Let me speak to Zonis."

"Yes, Commander."

"Ruth?"

"Yes, sir?"

"Do you confirm that six are missing against yesterday's tally?"

"Yes, Commander—if yesterday's tally was correct."

"What do you mean by that?"

Her voice sounded strained. "It is possible that Khelad is trying to discredit me."

"Yes, it is possible. It is also possible that the mines really are missing . . . Ahmed, continue with your programme. I'll be with you directly. Meanwhile, I will have one robot search the ship and one search the compound. Over and out."

Conrad called Matthew. "Did you monitor the conversation?"

"Yes, Commander."

"Detach two robots to carry out the required search."

"Decision noted, Commander. Execution proceeds. Paul is now searching the vessel, Peter is already in the compound. Query: if mines are discovered, are they to be returned to Mr. Khelad?"

"No, they are not! If the mines are discovered, the fact must be reported to me only. If they are linked for detonation, they must be neutralised. If they are not linked for detonation, they must remain where found."

"Decision noted," said Matthew imperturbably.

Thirty kilometres to the south, Lisa Uhlmann found a strange tree—or, more properly, the tree found her. Lieutenant Smith, piloting the hovercar, had just taken it on high life over about two hundred hectares of scrubland and had just reached a vast tract of prairie on which a herd of massive creatures oddly like the North American buffalo grazed.

Near the edge of the scrubland there was a single tree, very tall, with tendril-like branches hanging loosely and swaying in the light breeze. From a distance it had looked like a huge weeping willow. Indira wanted to observe the herd of grazing creatures, but felt that if she took the hovercar closer the sound of its engine might cause the creatures to stampede. Lisa wanted to go back and examine the strange tree. So far, nothing like it had been found on Tantalus.

Indira grounded the hovercar and glanced at the clock

on its instrument panel. "It's time we reported back to the *Santa Maria*. When we have done that, you can go and take a look at the tree, Lisa, and I will try to get closer to those meaty quadrupeds. It is beginning to look as if there is enough protein on Tantalus to supply all the colonists Earth can send."

They checked back with Matthew, reported their position, had it confirmed by the direction finder and then got out of the hovercar.

"We will rendezvous back here in thirty minutes, Lisa. O.K.?"

"Yes, Lieutenant."

"If either of us fails to make it, the other will carry out a limited search. If the one which is missing is not found before it is time to signal the star-ship again, the search will be temporarily abandoned and radio contact will be made on schedule. Further action will then be taken only on Commander Conrad's instructions. Is that clear?"

Lisa Uhlmann laughed. "Perfectly clear. I do not think there will be any problems, but one never knows. Am I permitted to take a laser rifle?"

"No, Lisa, you are not. You are aware of the Commander's standing orders. Until we find the saboteur—"

"Yes, Lieutenant, I know. I just thought you might be more reasonable. This reds under the bed syndrome is getting tiresome."

"Get moving, Uhlmann," said Lieutenant Smith coldly.

Lisa shrugged, turned and began to pick her way through the scrub towards the great tree. Indira watched her for a few moments. She did not like the rule that the new Expendables were not allowed to carry weapons when they were away from the protection of the compound. But she could appreciate the necessity. One laser rifle in the hands of a saboteur would be sufficient.

Presently Indira turned to make her way stealthily towards the grazing quadrupeds. Fortunately, she was down wind; so unless she made a lot of noise or frightened them by moving carelessly, she ought to be able to get quite close.

In fact, she got to within a hundred metres. Then she crouched in the grass and used her binoculars. The quadrupeds were strong, healthy beasts. Some of them—the males, probably—had a long single horn in the centre of the forehead. The biggest ones formed a protective ring around the rest of the grazing herd. That surely suggested that these creatures were the natural prey of some as yet undiscovered species. Indira did a sample count of a section of the herd and was able to estimate that the total number was about seven hundred.

All the creatures had long shaggy fleeces. So besides providing food for potential colonists, they would also provide wool. Indira was so engrossed in her observations that she was unaware of the passing of time. When, eventually, she glanced at her watch, she saw that she had only eight minutes in which to rendezvous at the hovercar.

Hastily she began to make her way back. One of the horned animals noticed her movement and let out an eerie bellow. Then, horn lowered, he charged with amazing speed. Indira was not afraid. She knew that, with her prosthetic legs, she could certainly out-manoeuvre and probably outrun the massive creatures. But she did not want to lead it or any of its fellows anywhere near the hovercar, which they might possibly damage.

She waited until the beast was almost upon her, then she sprang high into the air—a magnificent leap of three metres. The creature could not stop its charge. It hurtled on beneath her, only managing to pull up when it was about thirty metres past. By that time, Indira had landed safely and was crouching in the long grass. The animal turned, frustrated, no longer able to see any potential attacker. It pawed the ground, snorted nervously for a few moments, then ambled back to the herd.

Discreetly, Lieutenant Smith returned to the hovercar. She was six minutes behind rendezvous. But there was no sign of Lisa Uhlmann.

Indira waited two more minutes, peering across the scrubland. She could see nothing moving. She entered the hovercar, released one of the laser rifles from its magnetic lock, then went into the scrub, heading for the tall tree, to investigate.

She found Lisa Uhlmann. She found her pressed tightly against the trunk of the tree that from a distance had looked like a weeping willow. Her arms had been forced back, held by several green tendrils. Her legs had been forced open, also held by tendrils. Her fatigue dress had been torn and her full breasts exposed—tendrils gripped them. Tendrils had also ripped her trousers and entered her crotch. And one crimson-stained tendril had wrapped itself round her neck.

Lisa's eyes were closed, her mouth sagging open. Her breasts twitched and shuddered, but she did not seem to care, or be conscious of anything. Blood dripped from her neck, trickling slowly down her left breast.

Automatically, Lieutenant Smith moved forward to help her. As she did, a long tendril suddenly whistled out from the "tree" with the speed of a whiplash, wrapping itself tightly round one of her legs, tugging hard. She lasered it.

Then she stood well back and began systematically lasering the taut green strands that bound Lisa. The first she burned was the one round Lisa's neck. Blood dripped from the charred end of the tendril. Lisa's head fell forward on her chest.

One after another, the tendrils were severed. Lisa Uhlmann slumped to the ground like a torn rag doll. Indira resisted the temptation to go in and help her. The great tree still had a great many "weeping" green thongs, deceptively limp but hideously powerful. She set the laser on maximum burn. She couldn't blast the tree itself for fear of hurting Lisa; but she could and did burn the weeping tendrils.

She burned them ferociously. The green stuff hissed and crackled. Pungent black smoke rose up to the sky. When she judged that it was safe, Indira hurried to the unconscious woman.

Blood was still oozing from the wound in the neck. Lisa's body looked pale and shrunken. Carefully, Indira dragged her clear. Then she went back for the laser rifle. She was just about to burn the entire tree in sheer fury, but she stopped herself in time. It would be a senseless act. Kwango would doubtless want to look at it; and, anyway, her first duty was to her patient. There was plasma and an emergency medikit in the hovercar. By the look of things, Lisa Uhlmann was already desperately short of blood.

Somehow, Lieutenant Smith managed to hoist the unconscious woman over her shoulders to carry her in the fireman's lift position. Then she stood up. Her prosthetic legs took the strain effortlessly.

Lisa's head and limbs lolled slackly. More blood oozed from the wound in her neck. It couldn't be helped. It was too dangerous to leave her while Indira went for the medikit.

Indira began to run. She picked up speed. The legs moved with precision and power, like the wonderful machines they really were. Indira's greatest difficulty was not in supporting the weight but in keeping her balance. She ran faster than an Olympic athlete, leaping across low patches of scrub and landing perfectly. If anyone had witnessed the performance, they would have been dumbfounded.

Back at the hovercar, she lowered Uhlmann across the rear seat, got the medikit and set professionally to work. She cleared the neck wound, squirted it with the aerosol coagulant, then gave it a temporary coat of synthaskin. She listened to heart and breathing—weak, intermittent, critical. She gave a shot of adrenalin. Then she ripped Lisa's clothing still further and examined the rest of her. Weals on the waist, legs and shoulders—presumably where she had been gripped and pulled by the monstrous tree— bruises on the breasts, lower belly and vaginal area.

She listened once more to the heartbeat. It was stronger, but still erratic. The adrenalin was beginning to get through.

Lieutenant Smith climbed to the driver's seat and reached for the transceiver, broadcasting the distress call that had been recognised internationally for one and a half centuries.

"Mayday! Mayday! Hovercar to *Santa Maria*. Do you read me?"

"I read you." It was Matthew's imperturbable voice. "Also, I have your position. What do you require?"

"Hook me in to the Commander."

"Decision noted. Execution proceeds."

There was a brief silence. Then she heard Conrad's voice.

"What has happened, Indira? Are you O.K.?" She was gratified by the note of concern.

"I'm all right, James. Uhlmann had an accident. Get out here fast—and bring plasma."

"Willco. Out."

Conrad was in the chopper with plasma less than a minute after he had spoken to Indira. As he lifted, he wondered yet again why the prehensible robots had reconstructed the machine perfectly. But then, he told himself drily, God moves in mysterious ways.

Kwango and Pushkin were less than one kilometre from the ring system. They had encountered no opposition. They had also encountered little wildlife—which was not entirely surprising, since the sound of exo-skeletons crashing through the forest must have been heard by sensitive ears over a great distance.

Kwango said: "I can't understand it. We get so near, and nothing happens. If those clockwork monkeys are watching us—which I don't doubt, since eight metres of metal exo is hardly inconspicuous—they must assume, at best, that we are making a reconnaissance or, at worst, that we intend to attack."

Pushkin's voice crackled slightly. "There is some electromagnetic disturbance. I hear you, but reception is not good . . . Maybe somebody called off the dogs."

"How's that again?"

"I said maybe somebody called off the dogs, comrade."

"If they did, they had a reason, comrade. And it is probably one that we are not going to like. We have some good pix of the rings. Let's get the hell out."

"Wait!" Alexei pointed. On the denuded ground, about seventy metres ahead, there was a glint of metal. The sunlight turned it into a blinding mirror. Kwango thought it was hexagonal—like the indentations on the derelict starship.

"Shall we investigate, comrade?" asked Alexei. The static and the crackling was getting worse.

"No. It is all too neat. We'll get the hell out. Dat ole Kwango sixth sense tells me dat somethin' is brewin'. So we ain't going to stay for de big surprise."

But Pushkin appeared not to have heard him, or to have heard him and disobeyed, or to have heard something different.

He strode forward.

Kwango saw flashes in the sunlight.

"Down!" he shouted, flinging his own exo flat.

Pushkin either didn't hear or didn't care. The missile hit his exo-skeleton dead centre. It exploded, flew apart. Fragments of the exo-skeleton and bloody fragments of Pushkin come down like surrealist rain. Kwango was up and running before the pieces stopped falling. He ducked another missile and leaped high over a third. Then he went into overdrive, taking the exo back to the *Santa Maria* at seventy k.p.h.

Phase Five

CONRAD STIRS IT UP

Conrad's face was grim. He gazed sombrely at the four other Expendables sitting round the saloon table.

"How is the patient?" he asked Lieutenant Smith.

"Sedated. Apart from the neck, I can find no other wound. Heartbeat still rather weak, breathing somewhat shallow. I've given anti-biotics though there is as yet no trace of infection. Too early. I'll know more about that probably by the end of tomorrow . . . Uhlmann was in good physical condition. Unless we are very unlucky, she should be fit for light duty in about three days."

"We are already very unlucky," retorted Conrad, "if you want to call it that . . . Well, let us consider the state of play. We have lost a good engineer and an exo-skeleton, our chemist is out of action, and friend Khelad has lost six of his mines. All this in one day." He glanced fiercely at Ahmed Khelad. "The ship has been searched, the compound has been searched. Those damned robots have even gone through my personal locker. Not a trace . . . If I ever find you were playing funny games, Khelad, I personally will disassemble you. Are you sure six are lost?"

Ahmed sounded pained. "I am sure, Commander. I have no means of proving what I say, but I am sure."

"And you still think the culprit is Zonis?"

The Arab shrugged. "It gives me no pleasure to say yes."

"Commander," said Ruth, "does it not occur to you that Khelad's attitude has a historical precedent? For a long time it has been traditional for the Arabs to blame their own failures and short-comings on the Israelis."

Conrad sighed. "Propaganda is not relevant, Zonis. Facts are. Do you have any facts?"

She remained silent.

"Then listen to me, both of you," went on Conrad. "And listen good. Because of the new situation, we are going to have to crash the crash programme. How many mines have you got now, Khelad?"

"Three hundred and twenty."

"That is going to have to be enough—for the time being. Tomorrow, you and Zonis will start laying a random minefield round the defence perimeter. You will record their positions carefully and accurately. You will concentrate two thirds of your mines round the southern perimeter and one third round the northern."

"Boss," said Kwango, "the ring system is to the north."

"I know. You are supposed to be the resident genius. You work it out."

Lieutenant Smith said: "You think we will be attacked?"

"I know we will be attacked. The only question is when. Those monkey robots have proved that we are vulnerable. They took out Pushkin and his exo with the greatest of ease. Their intention to escalate is obvious. First they hit us with grenades, then they bring in powered missiles. Their programme suggests one overriding command: exterminate intruders regardless of cost . . . Well, if they can't achieve this in the next forty-eight hours, we will take the initiative. As for this so-called tree that trapped Uhlmann and drank her blood while putting her into happyland, we will make a study of its incidence and characteristics when we have dealt with the robots and the rings. The fact that it is not very prolific would indicate that it is not much of a problem . . . All right, let's break it up and get some sleep. Matthew is on the nav deck, supervising the defence system. Three armed robots are patrolling the perimeter, two are on board to take care of the fifth column. Kwango, see me in my cabin in five minutes."

Kwango took the drink that Conrad offered him. It was genuine Southern Comfort. He sipped it and savoured it with respect.

"Not from general stores," said Conrad. "That was shipped on my personal weight allowance." He poured himself a drink and gave a grim laugh. "Emergency rocket fuel. By the Lord Harry, I need it."

"Commander, you look dead tired."

"I am dead tired. I'm not as tough as I thought."

"How's the arm?"

"To hell with the arm, Kurt. I'm thinking of pulling out. And how do you like that?"

Kwango scratched his head. "Scuse me, Massa Boss. Seems like only yesterday I heard a man who looks just like you declarin' he was going for broke."

Conrad passed a hand wearily over his forehead. "I know . . . I know. Since then I have been thinking. We are expendable—but the *Santa Maria* isn't. It cost half the annual budget of a country like Israel to build it and put it here. Now that we are getting guided missiles thrown at us, have I the right to risk that kind of investment?"

Kwango was silent for a moment or two. Then he said: "The fail-safe mentality has its limitations. If we skip back to Terra with—metaphorically speaking—our tail between our legs, those Third World people are going to laugh themselves sick. When they recover from that, they will have ExPEND for breakfast. The money will be re-routed to buying tractors for people who don't know how to use them and wouldn't want to use them if they could . . . Kratos justified our existence, Boss. If we get smashed on Tantalus, it doesn't much matter. Mankind is already out of the Solar System. But if we prove Tantalus, those Third World people are going to curl up and send for the shrink. End of opposition to ExPEND—and, to put it fancifully, de laughing animal continues trekking gaily out to de stars . . . My, dat Southern Comfort sure is potent."

Conrad could not suppress a yawn. "You are right, Kurt. We have to go for broke. But if the *Santa Maria* does not return to Terra, the Third World people will probably get the programme smashed, anyway . . . Now, before I fall asleep and you get hit by the booze, give me another Kwango scenario. Make it sound optimistic. I've had enough bad news for one day."

Kwango grinned. "Boss, if I was to make it optimistic, you'd think it was science fiction. Why don't you get a good night's sleep, and we'll talk tomorrow?"

"Pour both of us another drink, then talk. That is an order."

"O.K. If that's the way you want it." Kwango fixed the drinks. "Apart from the ring system and nasty little robots that toss bombs and guided missiles, we know the planet is O.K. for man. The tree—or whatever it is—that had it off with Lisa while drinking her blood is fairly rare. No other specimen has been found growing in the area already surveyed. It is nothing more than a very so-phisticated, king-size Venus fly-trap. It's vulnerable. Wherever we find it, we can hit it at will. All we have to do is develop a kind of selective weed-killer. But if that is not possible—which I doubt—we simply do what Lieutenant Smith did: burn it."

Kwango took another sip of his Southern Comfort. "I am puzzled why we ain't seen no people. We get things thrown at us, but we don't meet any of the people who presumably don't want us around."

"There's an obvious answer to that," said Conrad. "They let their robots do the dirty work. Less messy."

"There's another answer," said Kwango, finishing his drink. "A nice simple one. There ain't no people. Or not many . . . If there were, we'd have been taken out before now."

Conrad was suddenly alert. "You could be right."

"It is customary," said Kwango. "And if there ain't no people, all we have done in touching down on Tantalus is to set off the burglar alarm and disturb the electronic dogs. Trouble is, we don't know how many dogs we have disturbed."

"We'll find out," said Conrad grimly. "Incidentally, there is one thing we don't have to worry about. I know where the missing mines are."

Kwango gazed at him astounded. "Then why the funny act with Khelad and Zonis? Now you really have them at cach other's throats."

"Precisely. Before, Ruth only suspected Ahmed. Now she thinks she knows for sure. Probably, Ahmed did not even seriously suspect her. But now he is convinced she is the saboteur. They watch each other like hawks. That way, they neutralise each other."

"Where are the mines, Boss?"

"I stowed them in the emergency escape hatch *after* it

had been searched. Now, let's get some sleep."

Kwango smiled. "Commander, you are a real mean bastard."

"Meaner than you think, black man. I have Uhlmann sewn up, too."

"Because she is sick?"

"No, because she will soon get better."

Kwango scratched his head. "Sometimes, I think I just don't understand you, Commander, sir."

"That affords some small satisfaction, Kurt . . . Now, let's get some sleep."

A BAD DAY FOR EXPENDABLES

Next day brought more trouble—some of it expected, some of it unexpected. In the morning, while Khelad and Zonis were busy laying the minefield, Kwango took the hovercar and reconnoitred to the south. He also had with him the robot, Peter, and two laser rifles. Specifically, he was looking for another of the bloodsucking trees that had almost taken care of Lisa Uhlmann.

Lieutenant Smith stayed in the *Santa Maria* to observe and attend to her patient. Under protest, and on Conrad's orders, she had shot Lisa full of a special stimulant. The wound was healing well, but Indira would have preferred to continue sedating her patient and ensuring that she rested for a few more days. Lisa did not know she had been given a stimulant. The needle went in while she was sleeping profoundly. She sighed in her sleep, and uttered a vague groan of protest. But that was all. The stimulant had been specially developed for the Space Service. It was the kind of wonder juice that could make a man or woman who had lost, for example, an arm, get up from the sick-bed and operate with superhuman energy for several hours. But, naturally, there was a price to pay later. Sometimes, it was death; but usually it was a nasty little once-off heart attack. Conrad knew all about the properties of Superform. He had been shot full of it a long time ago when he was still a full captain in the U.N.S.S. He had not cared too much for the subsequent heart attack; but it had been worth the precious time needed to take his vessel out of danger. He had explained the reasons for his decisions to Lieutenant Smith. He had also told her what to do when Superform began to take effect. And he had also given her a tiny, pill-sized gadget to insert in Lisa Uhlmann's neck dressing.

Meanwhile, Kwango found his tree. It was about thirty kilometres south-west of the *Santa Maria*, somewhat larger than the one described by Lieutenant Smith. But it was in much the same sort of situation—very close to a large tract of grassland where herds of herbivores roamed.

On the journey, Kwango had developed his own special investigation technique; and he had programmed the robot, Peter, with the necessary instructions.

First, an investigation was to be made of the area of ground at least fifty metres and not more than a hundred metres from the base of the tree. After that, Peter would approach the tree as closely as possible, armed with a laser rifle. Kwango would cover him from a safe distance and note the tree's response. The third test consisted of Kwango making the approach while Peter covered him.

The entire arrangement was very rough and ready; but Kwango was mindful that information about the tree was needed very quickly.

As he had expected, a careful search revealed the bones of many scattered animals. They lay in undergrowth, some covered by tall grasses and shrubs, many in various stages of decomposition.

A pattern emerged. The tree waited for its victim to approach within striking distance, then shot out its tendrils and dragged the creature in to suck from it the nutriment needed. When it had finished, the remains—

presumably nothing but skin and bone—were tossed as far away as the tree could manage so that future visitors would not be discouraged. Someday, if he had time, Kwango intended to analyse the ecological function of the shrubs surrounding the blood-sucking trees. He had a notion that they were symbiotic, depending on the tree for the materials that would keep them alive and healthy. Certainly, they had a great capacity for removing traces of tell-tale bones.

When Peter approached close to what later came to be called the ecstasy tree, it made not the slightest response to the robot's presence.

"Reach up and tug at one of those hanging fronds," called Kwango. He spoke much louder than necessary, trying to ascertain if the tree would respond to noise.

"Decision noted. Execution proceeds," returned Peter. "Query. Is it required that I detach a sample?"

"If there is no reaction to your pulling, detatch three samples, each one metre long, and return them to me."

"Decision noted."

There was no response to the robot's pulling. The tree appeared totally indifferent to Peter's presence, even when the robot methodically collected the required samples.

Kwango examined one of the specimens closely. It felt very strong and rubbery. In cross-section it looked almost like a miniature honeycomb, containing a number of tiny hexagonal tubes.

Kwango put the specimen down. "I am now going in close, Peter. You will cover me with the laser rifle. No matter what happens, unless you are sure that my life is in danger, you will take no action for forty-five seconds. If, as I expect, the tree takes hold of me in such a way that I cannot free myself, you will systematically laser whatever holds me. If I cannot then move myself, you will come in and retrieve me. Do you upnderstand?"

"Sequence understood, procedure understood. Decisions noted," responded Peter tranquilly.

Kwango made his approach. He did not get very far. When he was barely twenty metres from the base of the tree, the liana-like tendrils whipped out with fantastic speed and gripped him. At the same time, his laser rifle was torn from his hand, and within five seconds he was spreadeagled hard against the trunk, unable to move. He struggled, but only for a moment or two. He became aware of a sweet, overpowering scent; and the will to struggle died. He experienced pleasant sensations. The tree seemed now to be holding him gently, caressing him, stroking him, releasing strange voluptuous visions in his mind. He saw Ruth Zonis, naked, beautiful, beckoning. The world became deliciously dark . . .

The next thing he knew, he was lying flat on his back, blinking uncomprehendingly at the sky. He collected his wits—slowly. He was aware of a smell of burning. Peter was squirting something onto his neck.

"What the hell are you doing?" he demanded shakily.

"Cleaning the wound, sir, and applying a coagulant. It is only a very small wound. Query: shall I give it a film of synthaskin?"

"You do that," said Kwango, still not entirely in possession of his faculties. "Tell me later what happened." For the time being, he could only remember the haunting nearness and sexuality of Ruth Zonis.

"Decisions noted," said Peter. "Execution proceeds."

Kwango managed to sit up, and saw that nearly half the tree had been burned away.

Lisa Uhlmann was making a remarkable recovery. That much, Conrad had already ascertained from Lieutenant Smith who was with her in the sick bay. Uhlmann's temperature was back to normal, her blood pressure was good and the neck wound was healing nicely.

Conrad, having made his rounds, was sitting at the desk in his cabin. He had inspected the vessel and the compound. He had also been outside the stockade and assured himself that Khelad and Zonis were laying the minefield. The indefatigable Matthew was on the navigation deck at the communications console. All was well. The robots had their instructions—very precise instructions.

With Alexei's death, the problem of the potential saboteur had been simplified. Now there were only three to worry about. Khelad and Zonis were—temporarily, at least—neutralising each other. There remained the enigma of Lisa Uhlmann. It was all a question of timing . . .

Conrad reached a decision. He called Lieutenant Smith in the sick bay.

"I have just knocked my arm against the bulkhead. It has begun to bleed again—not much, fortunately. But there is a fair amount of pain. Can you come down to my cabin and look at the damage?"

"I'll be down in two minutes."

"Good. How is Lisa?"

"In great spirits. She has disposed of a very good breakfast. She will probably be fit for limited duty tomorrow . . . I'm on my way. Out."

When Lieutenant Smith reached Conrad's cabin, he said: "You left the laser rifle?"

"Yes."

"Do you think your actions seemed natural?"

Indira shrugged. "I hope so, but how can I know? I think you are wrong, James. I think you are wasting—"

Matthew's voice came over the intercom. "Commander, Miss Uhlmann has just lasered Luke and John in corridors A and C respectively."

"Message received, Matthew. Take no action."

"Decision noted."

Lieutenant Smith gazed at Conrad despairingly. "How could you know?"

He shrugged. "I didn't. I merely created the conditions for finding out."

Matthew came in again. "Miss Uhlmann appears to be making her way to your cabin, Commander. Do you wish her to be intercepted?"

"No, Matthew. Intercept only if she approaches a sensitive area as previously defined. Over and out."

Conrad took two small metal cubes out of his pocket. Each was a radio transmitter. Each had a button. One was red, one was green. He pressed the red button, and placed the transmitter on his desk. The other he held in his prosthetic hand. Then he turned to Indira and held out his injured arm. "Make it look authentic, Lieutenant. Inspect the damage."

While Lieutenant Smith was taking off the bandages, Lisa Uhlmann burst into the cabin. She held the laser rifle firmly, ready to burn them both.

"Uhlmann, what the hell are you up to?" asked Conrad angrily, affecting great surprise.

There was a wild look in Lisa Uhlmann's eyes. "Commander," she said icily. "I regret to report the party is over. You will never prove Tantalus. Believe me, I wish it were not necessary to kill; but there is no other way. The *Santa Maria* and all of us will stay on Tantalus. The

ExPEND project will be discredited. This, at least, gives the people of the Third World a fighting chance."

"So you are the one," said Conrad. He did not seem greatly perturbed.

"Yes, I am the one." She lifted one hand from the laser rifle for a moment and scratched nervously at the bandage round her neck.

"Just now you spoke of a fighting chance. That is exactly what you will be giving the Third World—in fact, all of Terra—if the ExPEND project is finished. Eventually, they will be fighting each other for land, raw materials, food."

She gave him a cold smile. "I am not going to be drawn into discussion. I regret this, but you and Lieutenant Smith have two minutes left. Use them for farewells, prayers, whatever you like. But don't plead. Otherwise, I will laser you instantly."

Conrad stood up. "Before Alexei Pushkin died," he said tranquilly, "I asked him to fit one laser rifle with an electronic override. This he did. The weapon was tested. You now hold it. It is useless."

Lisa Uhlmann was not to be shaken. "I would have expected better from you, Commander. I have just lasered two of your robots."

"I know. I hope they can be repaired. Now laser me."

Expertly she aimed for his forehead. Nothing happened. She pressed the stud again. Still nothing. She froze in bewilderment.

Conrad calmly reached for the tiny transmitter with the green button. He placed it close to the edge of the desk. "Lisa Uhlmann, I hereby charge you with mutiny, destruction of U.N. property and attempted murder. According to Space Regulations you will be tried by court-martial on

Terra when this mission is completed. Meanwhile, you
will be placed in suspended animation until this project is
completed."

"Damn you!" In rage and frustration, she flung the useless laser rifle at Conrad with all her force. Expertly, he
caught it with his prosthetic hand and placed it on the
desk by the transmitter.

Lisa Uhlmann turned to rush from the cabin. She never
made it.

Conrad pressed the green button.

She felt a stinging sensation in the side of her neck,
raised one hand feebly towards the bandage, then slumped
silently to the deck.

Indira knelt by her, checking heart-beat and breathing.
Finally, she looked up at Conrad. "Sometimes, James,"
she said heavily, "I think you, too, are a bloody robot."

"Compliments, compliments," said Conrad lightly. "Last
night, Kwango called me a real mean bastard."

"He was dead right—as always."

Briefly, Conrad's mask fell away. "I'm going to prove
this planet for colonisation, and I don't care what it costs
so long as I succeed." His voice seemed to have a cutting
edge. "Now, cut the subjective evaluations and get on with
your job, Lieutenant. Put Uhlmann in the cooler, then go
and tell Khelad and Zonis they can be nice to each other."

"Ay ay, sir." Indira's tone conveyed much sarcasm.
"What makes you think, mighty Caesar, that you can
command a cessation of the Arab-Israeli hostilities you
have encouraged?"

"Hate is a marvellous tool—if you know how to use it,"
observed Conrad. "Tell them I took the mines. They will
stop hating each other and only hate me."

But that was part of Conrad's calculations which came unstuck.

While the unconscious form of Lisa Uhlmann was being removed by the robot Paul, under Lieutenant Smith's supervision, back to the sick bay where she would receive a thorough medical check before being prepared for suspended animation procedure, Conrad ordered Matthew to investigate the condition of the two lasered robots.

Lisa Uhlmann had aimed well.

Matthew reported back: "Vizors and vision circuits in both robots completely destroyed, Commander. Breastplates punctured, memory banks have sustained heavy damage, power systems have sustained moderate damage. Luke's systems have suffered approximately seven point five per cent less damage than John's systems. With spare components from store and the facilities available, it is possible to recover one robot only. Recommendation: that Luke should be recovered."

"Recommendations accepted, Execute."

"Decision noted. Execution proceeds."

Meanwhile, having seen to the welfare of Lisa Uhlmann, Lieutenant Smith tried to raise Khelad and Zonis on the radio. She failed. She went to the nav deck and glanced at the screens. Neither of the Expendables was visible. But that in itself was not necessarily significant. The vids could not show what was happening immediately outside the stockade. The vid cameras were set at an angle that would allow at least fifty metres of dead ground.

Indira went outside to investigate. Pretty soon, she found Ruth Zonis.

Ruth was lying flat on her back, only half-conscious, her clothing torn, her face bruised and bloody, her legs wide open.

She could talk, but not too well. "Khelad raped me," she said thickly. "Maybe it was my fault. I don't know. Maybe I pushed him too hard." She raised herself a little and smiled weakly. "But, anyway, it must be clear he is the saboteur . . . Don't worry about me, Lieutenant. I'll live through it. Just get Khelad and take him out."

Indira stroked her hair. "Khelad wasn't the saboteur, Ruth. It was Lisa Uhlmann. Where is Ahmed?"

"I don't know. All the time, he was shouting wildly in Arabic." She gave a faint smile. "An Israeli woman is no match for an Arab male when he comes up from behind and hits her on the head . . . He is not in the compound?"

"No, he is not in the compound."

"Then he has gone over the hill, hasn't he?" Ruth sighed. "Three down. How are we going to prove Tantalus, now?"

"We'll prove it," said Indira fiercely. "No matter what it costs." Suddenly, she realised she was echoing Conrad's sentiments. She was strangely glad.

She reported back to him, telling him what she had found.

Then she turned to Ruth. "Can you get up and walk, or shall I send for a robot?"

"I can walk," said Ruth with great intensity. "No bloody Arab is going to have *that* satisfaction."

Phase Seven

KHELAD FALLS OUT OF A TREE

Conrad talked to Kwango. "How far are you away now, Kurt?"

"About fifty kilometres south-west. I had an intimate time with one of those things that tried to knock off Lisa."

"You hurt?"

"Not much. Anything been happening back home?"

"Not much," returned Conrad grimly. "Uhlmann lasered two robots, then came to burn me and blow the project. She's being readied for S.A."

Kwango let out a whistle.

"Don't do that over the radio," snapped Conrad.

"Sorry, Boss . . . She was the one. Now we can relax."

"Kwango, you have a talent for saying the wrong thing. Zonis has been raped by Khelad, and he has gone over the hill. Now get that thing on high drive and jet back fast. Find Khelad. We are two Expendables and one robot down. I want Khelad back before a clockwork monkey tosses him a present. By the way, the mine-field is laid. Make your approach to the stockade entrance tangentially; then you won't blow any of the things. You read me?"

"I read you, Commander. Is Khelad armed?"

"No. Not unless he thought to take a couple of mines. And even if he did he wouldn't want to carry them long."

"Boss, is Ruth O.K.?"

Conrad gave a grim laugh. "For a genius you are

pretty stupid. She can walk and she isn't screaming. But her face doesn't look too good and I don't think she'd like to play tennis. Move, Kwango! Get Khelad and don't make a mess of him."

"Ay ay, sir." Kwango felt the small wound on his neck. It didn't bother him too much.

From ten kilometres, Kwango began to spiral in towards the *Santa Maria*. He figured that ten kilometres was the most Khelad could have traveled. The ground favoured the hunted not the hunter. But, Kwango reasoned, Ahmed Khelad would probably be in a state of panic. Would he have enough nerve to lie still in the long grasses or, perhaps, climb a tree and hide in the foliage if the hovercar came near? Kwango thought not. He wondered if there was any way to increase the sense of panic and force the fugitive to break cover. He thought there was.

He turned to the robot, Peter. "What is your maximum speed on foot?"

"Query, sir: maximum speed for what terrain?"

"The terrain we are passing over now, stupid."

"Query, sir: why am I designated stupid?"

"Cancel statement, Peter. My mistake. Supply required data. The ground is firm but uneven, the grass is long. What is your maximum speed under such conditions?"

"Maximum speed estimated at eighteen kilometres per hour plus or minus seven point five per cent, allowing for variation of terrain."

"Then I will stop the hovercar and you will get out. You will take a laser rifle and you will proceed ahead of me and you will make zig-zag sweeps at an angle of forty-five degrees, each sweep to extend two hundred metres.

You will use the laser rifle only at my command."
Kwango stopped the hovercar.

"Decision noted. Execution proceeds." Peter got out.

The hovercar had a loud hailer. Kwango used it.
"Ahmed, I'm coming after you. So is Peter. He has a
laser rifle and he is programmed for homicide. If you don't
want to burn, surrender now."

Kwango put the statement on a loop replay at intervals
of fifteen seconds. The hovercar continued to spiral slowly
in towards the *Santa Maria* with Peter preceding it,
running tirelessly and methodically over the ground in the
appointed pattern.

Khelad was trapped less than four kilometres from the
stockade. Kwango almost ran him down. Ahmed leaped
up out of the grass directly ahead of the advancing hovercar. He raised his hands over his head, and he was
obviously shouting something. Kwango didn't hear what
it was until he grounded and got out of the hovercar.

"Don't let that bloody robot burn me, Kurt! Take me
to Conrad. Let me talk to him. That bitch Zonis brought
it all on herself. She taunted me and taunted me. She
wouldn't stop . . . All that stuff about Israelis being superior to Arabs . . . It got at my pride . . . I had to do
something . . . She is the saboteur, Kurt. She took the
mines."

"Ahmed," said Kwango calmly, "Ruth did not take the
mines. Conrad did. He wanted you both to watch each
other like snakes."

"Oh, my god!"

"Also, she is not the saboteur. Uhlmann is. Even now,
the good Commander has her routed for the cooler."

"Oh, my god!" repeated Khelad weakly. "Can I lower
my arms?"

"Yes, you light-skinned great-grandson of a slaver. You can do what you damn like. Conrad told me not to mess you up. But there is a destiny that shapes our ends, rough hew them how we will. Ahmed, my friend, you have just fallen out of a tree."

"Have I?" said Khelad, uncomprehendingly.

"That is what it looks like to me," said Kwango. Expertly he chopped Khelad in the throat. Then, even before the Arab could fall, Kwango kicked him in the crutch. When Khelad hit the ground, Kwango rolled him over and stamped on his belly. Then, almost as an afterthought, he smashed the flat of his hand down on Khelad's nose. Presently, when Ahmed Khelad could get his breath and stop groaning, he managed to vomit.

"I have some affection for Ruth Zonis," explained Kwango tranquilly. "That is why you fell out of a high tree. Under the circumstances, it is amazing that you didn't break any bones." He lifted the still retching Khelad to his feet. "Now, let's go talk to the good Commander. Feel free to tell him what you want. I shall not complain. It was worth it."

Conrad gazed at Ahmed Khelad, who swayed a little, dabbed at his swollen and still bloody nose, occasionally felt tenderly at his throat, his belly and his crutch. Ruth Zonis was present, as also were Lieutenant Smith and Kurt Kwango.

"So you still claim you fell out of a tree when the hovercar passed close by?"

"Yes, Commander. The approach was—was very unexpected . . . I panicked."

"Lieutenant Smith, do you think Khelad's injuries could be consonant with falling out of a tree?"

"They could be," said Indira carefully. "But it is unlikely." She glanced briefly at Kwango.

Conrad followed her glance. Then he turned to Khelad.
"Be that as it may. You are back. You are expendable,
Khelad—but you are expendable on my terms not on
yours. You are charged with rape and desertion. How do
you plead?"

Khelad shrugged, and let out a sigh. "Guilty."

"Have you anything to say in your defence?"

"What is there to say?"

"You could plead extreme provocation."

Suddenly Khelad drew himself up. "Commander, I do
not wish to plead extreme provocation. I have done stupid
things which I regret." He looked at Ruth Zonis, her face
still badly bruised, one eye swollen and almost closed.
"But I will not shame my race by showing cowardice."

Conrad said: "Then I find you guilty as charged. Before
I pass sentence, will anyone speak in defence of this
man?"

Kwango shook his head.

Indira remained silent.

Ruth Zonis said: "Yes, Commander. There are exten-
uating circumstances."

"What are they?"

"My reactions to Ahmed Khelad since we came to
Tantalus. It is common knowledge that I thought him to be
the saboteur. It is also common knowledge that I taunted
him and provoked him. He did dreadful things to me, and
I hope that, in time, the memories will fade . . . But I am
aware of my own responsibility, Commander—and of
yours!"

Conrad scratched his silver eye-patch irritably. "Zonis,
I must ask you to explain that final remark."

"You stole the mines," said Ruth Zonis coolly. "You deliberately increased the tension that already existed between myself and Ahmed Khelad. I appreciate your reasons; but that does not exonerate you from being an accessory to rape. Therefore, I submit that you are not competent to consider this case impartially."

Conrad gazed at her, open-mouthed. After a moment or two, he collected his wits. "Zonis, you are out of your mind!"

"Is she, Commander?" said Lieutenant Smith. "Is there no truth in what she has said?" Then she added with a faint smile: "Upon examination, I found Ruth Zonis to be in full possession of her faculties. Her attitudes and behaviour were entirely rational."

Conrad was astounded. "You, too!"

Indira was not to be intimidated. "I find her argument valid, that is all."

Conrad turned to Kwango. "Well, Kwango, are you also about to join this instant society for the protection of rapists and deserters?"

"Please," began Khelad. "I do not wish to cause any more—"

"Shut up!" snapped Conrad. "You've had your turn, Khelad." He gazed at the black man. "Well, Kwango. I'm waiting for you to utter."

Kwango shrugged, and glanced meaningfully at Ruth Zonis. "Include me out, Commander. I am an interested party."

"O.K., everyone, we have had the funnies. Now hear this. Whether you like it or not, here on Tantalus, I am the law—by virtue of the authority vested in me under U.N.S.S. Penal Code, Article Three . . . Ahmed Khelad, you have been charged on two counts: rape and desertion.

On the first count, my impartiality has been called in question. Therefore, I will suspend the charge until such time as you can be tried impartially. On the second count, I find you guilty. It being impractical to impose the statutory punishment of five years confinement at this time, this sentence is suspended until such time as you return to the Solar System. However, if during the rest of this mission your behaviour should prove to be exemplary, I will add a recommendation for clemency. These decisions will be recorded in the log."

"Thank you, Commander." Khelad dabbed at his nose.

"Thank me for nothing!" snapped Conrad. He turned to Kwango. "As for the tree with the black trunk which was responsible for making a mess of Khelad, contrary to order, I fine it—"

"One booze ration," said Kwango with resignation.

"Three booze rations," corrected Conrad maliciously.

"Thank you, Commander."

"Thank me for nothing . . . Now, you have all had fun —of one kind or another. The saboteur is in the cooler, so we can resume normal duty. Get some rest. You are going to need it."

Phase Eight

GO FOR BROKE

Although there were now only five operational Expendables and four operational robots, life was much easier; and, to Conrad, the future seemed fractionally more optimistic. It was now no longer necessary to guard the starship and the compound from attack from within as well as from without. Matthew had reported that one of the lasered robots would be operational in three more days. Major repairs, involving some "cannibalisation", had already been carried out. The time was needed mainly to test the circuitry, responses, audio-visual functions and mechanical co-ordination.

For this reason, and because Zonis and Khelad were still showing the effects of their different ordeals, Conrad decided to wait a few more days before he made an all-out attempt to crack the mystery of the rings. He wanted his personnel—both humans and robots—to be at optimum performance.

Meanwhile, there was work to be done. Kwango gave Lieutenant Smith, Zonis and Khelad advanced training in the use of exo-skeletons. Kwango was the expert. He could make an eight-metre, three-ton exo do things that Conrad had formerly believed impossible. In an exo, Kwango could run over good ground at nearly one hundred k.p.h. He could leap ten metres into the air or forty metres in a long jump. He could hurl fifty kilos of rock five hundred metres. Kwango was a phenomenon.

Pretty soon, his students got some glimmering of the Kwango technique. He had explained his secret.

"Once in harness," he said, "you've got to forget about your little bio-self. The exo magnifies you. It turns you into a temporary cyborg. Think big, feel through those metal limbs. When you get into harness, forget that you are a weak little animal. You have become god-like. Believe that those metal legs and arms are your legs and arms. Believe that you have almost inexhaustible sources of energy. You aren't you any more—you are super-cyborg—the god in the machine. When you achieve that kind of empathy, you will be able to feel through those metal fingers and feet. The atomic motors will become the motors that drive you and that you can command."

This, for Kwango, was a kind of poetry. Listening to the tirade, Conrad had been amazed. He had never suspected Kwango of indulging in such imaginative flights. But if that was the approach that paid off, then it was the right one.

Conrad wanted all of his diminished band to be expert in the use of exo-skeletons. Sooner or later, their lives and the success or failure of the expedition might depend on it.

Conrad's broken arm had mended nicely. Lieutenant Smith injected him regularly with something called Regeneron. It speeded up the process of metabolism and, consequently, the production of new cells. The main drawback was that it made the patient almost incessantly hungry for fats and proteins. Also, it slightly accelerated the ageing process. Neither of which bothered Conrad greatly. He was perfectly happy to eat large helpings of Terran steak and fat, and he was not greatly concerned about the prospect of a minimally premature senility. He thought the odds were that he would die with his boots on. After all, he was the first, the very first, Expendable.

It was a great relief not to have to worry any more about sabotage. Now, Conrad could give his whole mind to the problems of Tantalus. Of course, he reflected, now that the sabotage thing had been sewn up, there was no reason why the crash programme should be continued. Except that if he took it more slowly, the chances were that there would be more casualties. Those bomb-throwing, missile-happy little robots would find other opportunities to take someone out. Conrad did not want to accept any more losses.

While the robot Luke was being made operational, it was Conrad's intention to confine all activity to within the defence perimeter. There was plenty of work to occupy Zonis, the biologist; and Khelad had been instructed to design and manufacture a radio-controlled laser battery which could be mounted on a high platform in the compound and used to dominate the terrain outside up to a radius of one point five kilometres. When Kwango was not engaged in exo-instruction, he was either helping Zonis, or collating and running various Kwango scenarios through the computer. Conrad himself had enough administrative work to keep him fully occupied. Lieutenant Smith was the only one with a little time on her hands. She used it to catch up on much lost sleep.

All went well until the late afternoon of the second day, when the light was beginning to fade and the fiery ball of Regulus was about to sink over the western horizon.

The indefatigable Matthew, on duty at the screens on the nav deck, reported to Conrad: "Commander, there is considerable movement outside the defence perimeter

Range one thousand two hundred metres approximately. A number of entities, recently designated as prehensile indigenous robots, are approaching the defence perimeter. Provisional estimate of number thirty plus or minus twenty to forty per cent. It is difficult to evaluate because—"

"What direction?" asked Conrad.

"From the planetary west."

"At this time of day, it would be. How much daylight have we left?"

"Approximately eleven point three minutes S.E.T."

"Sound action stations."

"Decision noted, Execution proceeds."

Conrad had already planned for just this contingency. Everybody knew where to go, what to do.

Kwango was into his exo-skeleton and harnessed within one minute. Khelad took nearly forty seconds longer.

Conrad called them by radio. "Get out over the eastern section of the perimeter. Take lasers. Circle wide and come directly behind them, but don't open up until they do. Then burn anything that moves. We'll try to keep their attention. Over and out."

Believing that an attack might come by night, Conrad had required the robots to erect a system of floodlights which could be used to illuminate all the ground outside the perimeter to a range of five hundred metres.

Meanwhile, Conrad ordered the robots to make the vessel ready for lift-off if the perimeter defense were seriously breached; and Ruth Zonis and Lieutenant Smith armed with lasers, took up positions near the base of the torus. They could, upon command, withdraw into the *Santa Maria*. Conrad took over from Matthew on the nav deck.

The light was fading; but he did not want to switch on the floodlights until he had to. He was not sure how long they would last before they were taken out.

Conrad glanced at the screens. Kwango and Khelad were successfully away and fading into the darkness. They were going at great speed, but it would be at least three or four minutes before they could come up behind the attackers.

The tiny robots made good use of the cover and the fading light. Fortunately, there was no wind, so where grass moved, it was safe to assume that a robot was moving, too. Conrad reassessed their number at between forty-five and fifty-five. He hoped he was right. But, for all he knew, this could simply be a diversionary assault with a larger force poised to strike from another direction.

The battle opened with enemy casualties.

The first attackers had reached Khelad's minefield. There were two simultaneous flashes of light followed by another. Conrad was amazed at what he saw. Fragments of the tiny robots rose high into the air. Evidently the mines were considerably more powerful than he had originally required. He was devoutly grateful. But later, Khelad would have to explain.

The attack was halted temporarily. Conrad took advantage of the lull to establish contact with his four Expendables.

"Kwango, how goes it?"

"We are five kilometres away from the stockade. No contact established. Something tells me they, too, are going for broke. We are about to sweep round and should come in behind them about five minutes from now."

"Warn me when you are ready to strike."

"O.K. Boss. Out."

"Indira?"

"Yes, James."

"All well?"

"Yes. What were the explosions?"

"Khelad's mines. He made them one hundred and forty proof. You are sure of your retreat procedure?"

"Yes."

"How's Ruth?"

"In good shape, Commander." It was the voice of Ruth Zonis. "Israeli women are tough. Don't forget that."

"I won't . . . Recall procedure. If I signal retreat, drop it all and get into the *Santa Maria* fast. Got that, Lieutenant?

"Yes, Commander."

Then the fun started. The tiny robots, evidently, had now worked out what a mine-field was and what its function was. They tossed grenades before them as they advanced. The Starbursts registered on the command screens. It was, thought Conrad, like Guy Fawkes Night or the Fourth of July.

A missile suddenly blew a great hole in the defence perimeter. It was followed by another missile making an even larger hole.

Christ, thought Conrad, they are getting ready for the big rush.

"Smith?"

"Yes, Commander."

"Cover the starboard gap."

"Ay ay."

"Zonis."

"Yes, Commander."

"Take the port, Burn anything that moves."

"Kwango."

"Yes, Boss."

"Where the hell are you, now?"

"Right behind the little ones, Boss. Range one thousand metres."

"Are you ready to come in?"

"Yes, Boss. Both ready and willing."

"Good. They have breached the stockade. Attack expected imminently. I am now going to switch on the lights. I doubt if you'll have more than forty seconds before they are taken out. Start moving, genius—and start burning."

Indira reported. "Some have reached the gap, James. I can't see too clearly, but I think they are trying to set up some kind of machine."

"Missile launcher, I expect," returned Conrad. "Take it out, if you can. I'll give you some light; but you won't have it for long, I think."

There was another blast; and another great hole appeared in the wall of the stockade. The *Santa Maria* quivered like a living thing.

It was now or never, thought Conrad. "Lights on!" he radioed and hit the switch.

The floodlights blazed into life. The sudden illumination revealed an amazing sight. There had been far more of the tiny robots than Conrad had suspected. They had several missile launchers; and they were working coolly, methodically, regardless of casualties.

The terrain outside the stockade was dotted with craters where mines had exploded or had been exploded by bombs. Indira and Ruth were pouring laser beams through the breached stockade; and, strangest sight of all, the two great exos operated by Kwango and Khelad were streaking in from the outer darkness like silver giants.

Kwango was among the astonished robots first. He lasered half a dozen before they were aware of his presence. Then he took a mighty leap and landed precisely on top of two of the monkey robots who were hastily swivelling a missile launcher in his direction. He literally stamped the lot into the ground.

"I am de U.S. Cavalry," he announced to no one in particular, as he lasered another missile group.

Khelad followed close with similar devastating effect. But he was unlucky. A missile blew one of his exo-legs off. He fell down and lasered more robots from the ground for a moment or two. Then, somehow, he got up and started hopping.

Conrad was amazed to see that some of the Kwango magic had rubbed off on Ahmed Khelad. Wherever he hopped, a robot or robots were flattened into the ground.

"The breaches are clear," reported Lieutenant Smith.

One floodlight erupted in a gout of flame and died.

"Advance and support Kwango and Khelad."

Another floodlight was taken out.

"Matthew, take over up here. If the vessel is endangered, lift into orbit."

"Decision noted. Execution proceeds."

Matthew came up to the nav deck as Conrad grabbed a laser rifle and hurried down to the entry-port. He was dirtside almost before Matthew was at the screens.

Two floodlights remained. One died almost as soon as Conrad had joined Indira and Ruth at the largest breach.

Khelad was still hopping about—devastatingly. Kwango had had both his exo-arms blown off. But, unlike Khelad, he was still busy stamping the enemy into the ground.

"Lieutenant, Zonis, cover them," said Conrad. "Pretty soon the last light will be out and they will be in trouble."

Then he radioed: "Kwango, Khelad, you are recalled. Return to the stockade with all possible speed. Support Zonis and Lieutenant Smith in defence of *Santa Maria*. Acknowledge."

"We are having fun!" protested Kwango.

"When the last light dies," snapped Conrad acidly, "you will have more fun than you can handle. Execute!"

"Decision noted," said Kwango in a dreadful imitation of Matthew. "Execution proceeds . . . Come on, Ahmed. The boss is turning chicken."

"What next?" asked Indira, with a sudden premonition.

Conrad closed his eye. Then he removed the silver patch that covered his infra-red eye and placed it over the bio-eye. He felt giddy for a moment or two as he registered everything with totally different colour values. He saw red, black, blue and white in the strangest places.

"What the hell do you think? When the glory boys have got back, I am going out to mop up. There can't be more than ten or twelve of those things still operating."

"Then we are safe," said Indira. "Wait until daylight."

"We are not safe, and I don't need daylight."

Kwango executed a marvelous leap over the stockade before the last floodlight died. Khelad was less lucky. His hop wasn't high enough. He hit the top of the stockade and fell flat. He was temporarily stunned.

Darkness prevailed.

"Now hear this," radioed Conrad. "As of this moment, Lieutenant Smith has assumed command. I am going out to deal with the surviving attackers. It is my intention to pursue and destroy. In the event that I do not return, Lieutenant Smith will decide whether to continue or abandon the proving of Tantalus on the evaluations of

Mr. Kwango. Meanwhile the defence of the *Santa Maria* is top priority. Over and out."

"James Conrad, you are a very stupid man!" stormed Indira.

"Yes, love. But that is hardly news." Conrad moved quietly through the breach. It was now so dark that Lieutenant Smith didn't even see him go.

But it was no longer dark to Conrad. It was a glowing world of brightness and blackness and strange, shimmering hues. Craters, still retaining the heat of bomb and mine explosions, looked like rippling bright pools. Fragments of hot metal glowed weirdly.

Conrad moved slowly, with great care and stealth. A few steps away from the breach, he turned and looked back. Indira was still there. The telltale glowing of her eyes and lips, even her breasts and her crutch radiated hazily through the darkness. Conrad devoutly hoped that the alien robots did not have infra-red circuits.

It was as if she had heard his thought, because abruptly she disappeared.

Conrad stood quite still, laser rifle ready and gazed intently around him. About fifty metres away a bright pattern moved. A bright pattern of fifteen variable stars. He watched them move for a moment or two. Then, mentally, he joined up the bright points just as when he was a child long ago he had joined up numbered dots in a puzzle book to make a picture. He made the picture. It was humanoid with a tail. The heat came from power source, and, presumably, limb motors. He lasered it accurately and flung himself flat. The monkey robot disintegrated instantly and noisily with a brief flash showing fragments gouting into the air. He must have hit the power source.

The destruction triggered more movement. Two more

sets of fifteen variable stars moved through the darkness towards the stockade.

Conrad lasered them both. Both fell apart. No explosion. No flash. They just fell apart.

Missed the power source, thought Conrad. It didn't matter. The robots had been taken out. Their stars were fading in the now dewy grass.

He stayed still for several minutes. He could see no further movement. He decided to make his way—very slowly—round the entire stockade.

He took out one more robot before he had travelled fifty paces. As before, he lasered and dropped flat. Three lemons. He had hit the power source again.

The jackpot came about two hundred paces later. Five star-patterns manipulating something that glowed very brightly. Missile and launcher, perhaps. Conrad watched, fascinated, almost hypnotised. His brain was trying to make sense of the data; but it was all very confusing. He shook himself out of the trance. Range twenty metres —or was it thirty? Or was it forty? What the hell! Laser the bastards anyway.

He went for broke. He lasered the bright glow. There was the most godalmighty explosion. Before he could hit the ground, James Conrad, D.S.S.C. and bar, Grand Cross of Gagarin, was lifted high by the shock wave and smashed down fifteen metres from where he had stood.

The party was over. He gave a great sigh, tried to stand up, felt arrows of pain everywhere, fell flat, tried desperately to remain conscious—and failed.

WINNER TAKES ALL—THE FINAL SCENARIO

Once more Conrad woke up in the sick bay. Once more he had his bio-arm strapped up; and, for a bonus, there was some needlework on his forehead, face and shoulder. He felt himself gingerly, felt what he could move comfortably and what he couldn't. His neck hurt, his shoulder hurt, his face hurt and—goddammit—his bio-arm hurt abominably. He was a mess.

"Welcome home, Boss."

There was a fuzzy black shape looming over him. He tried very hard to focus. Finally, he made it. He saw Kwango's great, toothy smile.

"How long have I been out?" His voice sounded thin and reedy. Christ, thought Conrad, I am a bloody mess.

"Best part of two and a half days. Commander, you sure use up plasma at one hell of a rate. Anyone would think you were hooked on the stuff." Kwango glanced at the drip feed by the side of the bed. "Haw, haw. I think I made a funny."

Conrad tried to smile, felt a searing pain in his cheek, and hastily cancelled the gesture. The pain continued for a while and was followed by a nasty throbbing sensation. It was some seconds before he could speak.

"Kwango, do me a favour," he said, moving his lips as little as possible and slurring the words. "Don't try to make any more funnies for a while. It hurts."

"Sorry, Boss. I'm clever but stupid."

"Where is Lieutenant Smith?"

"The temporary Commander," said Kwango pointedly, "is about her duties of temporary commanding. Want me to call her?"

"No. Is the *Santa Maria* secure? Have the breaches been fixed? Have there been any more attacks?" Every word was painful to utter, and Conrad thoroughly detested the weak, old man's voice that uttered them. But there were things he had to know.

Kwango said simply: "Rest easy, Boss. Everything is O.K. The war is over. Tantalus is ours for the taking."

Conrad was confused. He tried to digest the information, but it didn't make much sense.

"Kwango, I want facts!" He managed to get a tone of command into the weak voice, but the effort cost him dearly. "I may be smashed up, but my brain still functions. What has been going on?"

Kwango sighed. "Boss, I got problems. You are full of holes that had to be sewn up, you lost a lot of blood, you've been through an adrenal crisis that would have killed anyone less stubborn—no offence, you bust your arm yet again, you've got tenosynovitis—so the good Lieutenant says, and for all I know you probably got morning sickness as well . . . Lieutenant Smith is a hard woman. She says if I say anything to upset you, excite you, exhaust you or make you anything less than relaxed and happy, she will use those lovely prosthetic legs of hers to stamp every bone in my body into agricultural fertiliser."

"Kwango, you now have another problem," said Conrad grimly. "If you don't give me the information I require, I promise you that when I rise from this bed I will strangle you so slowly with my prosthetic arm that you will bitterly regret not being turned quickly into fertiliser."

The big negro rolled his eyes. "O.K. Boss, take it easy. But if Lieutenant Smith does her thing, I'll haunt you for ever . . . You want the whole story now, or the headlines first?"

"Headlines first. Then tell it like it was from the time I got hit by an earthquake."

"Fasten your seat-belt, Commander. The bad news: Khelad is dead. The good news: there ain't no ring system any more, there ain't no monkey robots. And, incidentally, the computer says that derelict space vessel won't rendezvous with Tantalus again for about one hundred and sixty-eight years.

"Now grab this on-the-spot report brought to you live by our special investigator on Tantalus. The night Commander James Conrad heroically faced unknown numbers of alien robots in a reckless attempt to ensure the safety of—"

"Kwango!"

"O.K. Commander. I forgot. Cool it . . . When you went out through the breach, we took up defensive positions. Lieutenant Smith went topside to see what she could see on the screen—which wasn't too much. She got the flash when robots were being lasered, and knew you were still operating. Then came the big boom—and after that nothing but blackness. I thought of going out after you in the exo; but unless I used the exo's floodlight, it wouldn't have been much good. And if I did use the light, I'd have been a lovely target. Anyway, the Lieutenant smashed the idea, much to my relief. She said to wait thirty minutes before taking any further action.

"It was a long thirty minutes. The screen dark, and nothing but silence. Finally, I tried again to persuade

her to let me take an exo. She didn't buy it. Then Khelad
came up with a more persuasive idea. Said he had good
night vision and was used to operating in the dark. Didn't
say how or where he had gained this useful experience.
Just volunteered to go out and snoop around. Nobody
thought of anything better. So he went—with a blacked
coverall, a laser rifle and a head lamp. We had pin-pointed
exactly where the big bang was. So he went straight to it,
snaking on his belly through the grass. Didn't meet no
opposition. Snooped about some more. Eventually bumped
into you, more dead than alive, and brought you in.

"Bastard Arab rapist that he was, I could have kissed
that boy. A strange character, that Ahmed. Very droll. He
said to Ruth: 'Have I at last done something that you will
not despise?' *Very* droll . . . Anyway, the good Lieutenant
took one look at you and saw that she was going to have a
hell of a fight, cheating the Devil. So she put me in command and whisked you off to Intensive Care . . .

"Boss, you were a one-man disaster area. You were
covered in blood and you looked like you had been taking
a joyride in a garbage reducer. I bet Lieutenant Smith one
booze ration you wouldn't last six hours."

"You didn't have any booze ration to bet," said Conrad
thickly.

Kwango shrugged. "I know that, Boss. You know that.
But women are very stupid. She just slapped my face—
hard enough to rattle the marbles—then marched off and
worked on you like a whirlwind . . . Desired effect. I am
a very cunning chess player . . . Well, came the dawn.
And you were still alive—against all the odds. And we had
not been attacked again—against all the odds.

"At first light, I sent Khelad out in an exo. He had some
talent for using an exo, despite being an Arab. He found

nothing but fragments of knocked-out robots. All was sweetness and tranquility. After a time, I went out to take a look from ground level. Commander, I got the big surprise. Some of the robots only had one arm, some didn't have any tails, and a couple only had one leg each."

"So?" said Conrad. "They were lasered or blown off by mines."

"That is the point, Boss. They weren't. The stumps were covered with that regenerative bio-skin that got Ruth all excited. It was easy to tell which robots were damaged by us. The joints were smashed, the bio-skin ripped, and all the engineering and wiring was exposed . . . I counted fifty-seven wrecked robots, including sixteen of the incomplete ones. There must have been at least another ten utterly fragmented. All of which, Commander, led to some very interesting thoughts."

"So it would seem," said Conrad thoughtfully, oblivious of his pain. "If they had to throw incomplete robots at us, they must have scraped the bottom of the barrel. Right?"

"Right. The robots that couldn't function efficiently would at least be useful as distractions—targets for our fire while the others mounted the attack. It was the end sequence in a game of military poker. Cards face down, winner takes all."

"Still no people," mused Conrad.

"Boss, there never were any people," said Kwango. "Like I said, there were only the robots stacked against us—and the rings. And now both are busted. And while you been sleeping off your excesses, I did a survey from the chopper and only found seventeen ecstasy trees in one thousand square kilometres. So they present no problem. We can burn them if we want to, and Ruth is also developing a chemical poison . . . For the rest of the planetary cycle, we can be tourists. By the time the first colonists come through—"

"Cut the lullaby and get on with the briefing," said Conrad. Talking was a great effort. "How was Khelad taken out?"

"It goes like this," went on Kwango. "After I'd looked over the smashed robots, the conclusion was obvious. No people, no repair facilities. Whatever that goddam ring system might be, it was just like an old-fashioned clock, running down and with no-one to rewind it . . . After I'd told Lieutenant Smith the score, Khelad and I got her permission to go take a look. We used exos and we carried lasers. Also, Ahmed had knocked up some potent plastic explosive in case we needed to blast our way in.

"We went to the place where Alexei and I found that trapdoor set in the ground. I figured it was maybe an underground entrance to the rings. I figured right.

"There were no handles, so we couldn't pull the door open. We tried lasering it, but we didn't win. Ahmed unharnessed from his exo and placed the explosive with a thirty-second detonator. Then we stood back and waited for de big boom. The door blew. When the dust had settled, Ahmed with a big grin on his face, claimed the right of first entering."

Kwango shrugged. "Hell, Boss, the man had done good works. He brought you back alive, and he'd just blown the door. Anyway, I let him go. Sad mistake. Ten seconds after he went down the passage, there was one godalmighty blast and he came hurtling back like the daring young man in the circus cannon. He went up high and hit the deck hard. He was D.O.A., Boss—what was left of him. Before I could take a good look at him—which was not something I wanted greatly—the entire ring system blew . . . I was lucky to still be in my exo. Fifty kilo chunks of debris came raining out of the sky. I got flattened by the blast; and when I woke up, I had to dig my way out of a pile of debris."

"Booby-trap," said Conrad.

"Yes, Commander."

"The infallible Kwango goofed."

"Yes, Commander."

"Kwango, you are too bloody clever."

"Yes, Commander."

Conrad was sweating with pain and exhaustion. The sweat began to trickle down into his eye. "Wipe my forehead, man—and be careful of the needlework. Then get on with your report."

"Yes, sir." Kwango dabbed gently with some cotton wool. "I'll make it fast, Boss, because you don't look too good. After that, I call the Lieutenant. O.K.?"

"No."

"Then I call her now."

"Kwango, I gave you an order!"

"As of now, you don't give orders. You are just a bust-up piece of wreckage, Commander, sir, that the Lieutenant snatched back from the Devil with some very fancy surgery. But so you won't bust a blood vessel and ruin her work, I'll give it to you fast.

"The ring system was a town, Boss. But not like you and me think of a town. One of the rings was a sort of museum/art gallery. Artifacts, pictures on the wall. All that stuff. This I found out when I poked in the ruins and started to put a few bits and pieces together. Another of the rings was a vast dormitory, and another was a complex of lab/workshops. Then there was a ring where they lived and ate and maybe had some fun. And there was part of a ring where they reared kids and educated them. The last ring was, I think, the power house. But I'm not too sure.

"Boss, these people were very anthropomorphic. That is why the robots had prehensile tails. They were made to look exactly like their masters.

"Now comes the big joke. These tailed people had a very sophisticated culture. I don't know too much about physics; but their metals and plastics are way ahead of ours. They had a written and recorded language which our computer is now working on. But, most important, they told their history in pictures. I poked about in the wreckage of the art gallery long enough to put some of it together—enough, I think.

"The joke is this; Commander. The ring system was a refugee camp. And how do you like that?"

"A refugee camp?" Conrad was incredulous. "What the devil do you mean?"

"Political refugees. They came to Tantalus to establish first a settlement—the rings—then most likely a new civilisation. On their own planet, they were second class citizens. Haven't yet figured out where their planet is. Their star maps are different from ours, so it's got to be a heap of light-years away. The computer is working on that, too.

"Anyway, Boss, this is the final scenario. Hundreds of years ago—it's got to be hundreds because of the rate of oxidisation of their metals—these people came to Tantalus and used the materials of their space ship to begin the ring system. The ring shape seems to have some symbolic value for them—maybe something like the Christian halo. But, somehow, they were followed by the bad boys in that king-size derelict egg upstairs. There was a shoot-out. Nobody won. The surviving robots must have had some kind of programme built into their circuits to maintain the rings for, maybe, a second coming.

"That's why they got uptight when we came out of the sky. We were not what the robots expected. Maybe they figured we were the enemy, so they tried to take us out."

Conrad was exhausted, but his brain still functioned—after a fashion. "How the hell was my chopper knocked out?"

Kwango shrugged. "Can't say, Boss. But those people surely had a good defence system, otherwise they couldn't have blasted the super egg. Maybe it was winding down. Maybe you should have been vapourised. I just don't know . . . We'll have to wait till some bright boys from Terra figure out all the details . . . You want the cream of the joke, Commander?"

Conrad said: "Wipe the bloody sweat away."

Kwango obliged. "You feel better?"

"No, I feel terrible. Now give me the funny. I think I can take one and one only . . . You were right. I'm mincemeat. After you have uttered, call Lieutenant Smith and make your peace with God."

"The cream of the joke, Commander, is that the refugees had yellow tails, and their oppressors had black tails . . . There is nothing new under the sun."

Conrad smiled, and hurt himself dreadfully. "You stupid black bastard," he mumbled.

"Whitetrash," retorted Kwango equably. "Your superiority complex hasn't done you much good, has it, Commander?"

But Conrad wasn't listening. He was unconscious.

Lieutenant Smith came in. She glanced at her patient,

then she gazed at Kwango. "What the hell have you been doing?"

"He's a very obstinate man, Lieutenant. He wanted the full story."

"And you gave it to him?"

"Yes, maam."

"You're a fool, Kwango."

"Yes, ma'am."

"And don't call me ma'am ever again. You are fined—"

"One booze ration?"

"Your entire supply," she snapped furiously. "Now get out before I give you a drop-kick that will knock you through the bulkhead."

"Yes, Lieutenant." But Kwango didn't go. He stayed while Indira checked Conrad over. "How is he?"

"He'll live," she said grimly. "He'll live to wish he hadn't." Suddenly, she smiled. "You and he are very much alike, Kurt. Despite the obvious differences, both of you are brilliant, resourceful and loyal."

Kwango gazed at her in amazement.

"You are also small boys, heavily disguised as big stupid idiots."

"Lieutenant, there is one important difference," said Kwango with dignity. "I have some feelings for my fellow men, but that mean bastard just doesn't care—so long as he delivers."

Conrad opened one eye blearily. "I heard that," he said. "Kwango, I fine you—"

"Boss, you can't hurt me no more. De good Lieutenant has just broken me."

Indira smiled. "Kurt, go pour yourself a double Scotch. You look as if you need it."

Kwango's mouth fell open. Finally he managed to speak. "But you said—"

"Medical prescription," retorted Indira. "You are in a state of shock."

Kwango grinned. "Lieutenant, I never been more shocked in my life."

MISSION ENDS

Conrad, looking bronzed and very fit, stood by the side of a large steel box which had been carefully set up by the robots Matthew and Mark in Pushkin Square in the small log-cabin town of Kheladelphia. As yet, Kheladelphia possessed no citizens. But they would come. Soon they would come. They would come one at a time out of the matter transmitter, each in a titanium cylinder that was an independent suspended animation unit.

Conrad had never been able to understand how the matter transmitter worked, though Matthew had tried to explain the theory of sub-spatial matter transmission. Matthew was fully conversant with both theory and practice. He had seen it all, done it all before. Conrad remembered briefly that dramatic moment when the first colonist had rolled through on Kratos. A doctor. Dr. John Whatsis-name. Well, it didn't matter what his name was. Even now, no doubt, he was carrying out his duties in a thriving town on a recently colonised planet on the other side of the sky . . .

Still, this matter transmission was an unnerving pheno-menon. Conrad knew he would never get used to it, never understand it. The important thing was that it worked. The white man's magic. How else could it be described? You could chill somebody on Terra, fifty-six light years away, then have him pop out in a titanium sausage on

Tantalus, ready for resuscitation. The white man's magic . . .

Also present with Commander Conrad were Lieutenant Smith, Kurt Kwango and Ruth Zonis. The surviving Expendables. They had earned their right to be present at the first arrival. They had made it all possible.

It seemed a long time now since the monkey robots had made their death-or-glory attack on the *Santa Maria*. It was a long time. It was more than nine-E-months. Since then, much had been accomplished. The rest of the planet had been surveyed. The entire surface had been subjected to photographic and magnetometric analysis. Rich deposits of iron, bauxite, manganese and copper had been discovered. The existence of oil fields had been proved. The oceans were teeming with various types of fishes, many suitable for human consumption.

And, finally, Kheladelphia had been built—twenty kilometres south of the dead ring system. So here was a planet where mankind could have another chance . . .

Conrad remembered vividly the building of Kheladelphia. Everyone had taken part in it—the four Expendables and the robots. The Expendables, in their exo-skeletons, had uprooted the trees and shaped the logs, the robots had trimmed them to size. Then the town had been laid out—a simple plan. Four main streets: North Street, South Street, East Street, West Street—all meeting at Pushkin Square. Then the houses, the storage chambers, the hospital and the school had been built.

It was Ruth Zonis who had named the town Kheladelphia. She did not give her reasons. No one asked for them. But Conrad understood.

Now he gazed at the large steel box as if hypnotised. It has its own built-on atomic generator to produce the fantastic voltage for the receiving field. It also had a vacuum-sealed door.

There was a great hiss as all air was pumped out of the receiving chamber.

"Reception sequence one commencing," said Matthew. "All systems normal. Molecular echoes matching pattern equation. Sequence begins. All systems still normal. Physical resolution now begins. All systems continue normal."

The Expendables gazed intently at the matter receiver. There was no external change. But inside the evacuated black box a miracle was happening. Matter—metal, flesh, bone, blood—that had burst through the barrier of light-years as a fantastic blast of sub-spatial radiation was now resuming its normal form.

"Well," said Conrad, trying to make his voice sound matter-of-fact, "pretty soon we'll have company."

Ruth Zonis stood close to Kwango and shivered, though the air was warm. Kwango put an arm round her protectively. "Take it easy, Ruth. This is how we shipped them in on Kratos. It works."

Zonis and Kwango had had something going for quite a time now, thought Conrad. He hoped they gave each other some pleasure. They had worked hard.

"I wish—I wish," said Ruth, "that Ahmed and Alexei could be here." She looked at Kwango nervously, then added: "Just at this moment, I mean."

Conrad raised an eyebrow, glanced at Lieutenant Smith and shrugged. But Indira knew what she meant. So did Kwango.

"Little one, they are here," he said gently. "They helped to make it possible."

"Physical resolution completed," said Matthew. "All

systems normal. Unit one ready for disposal. Instructions required."

"Open the chambers," said Conrad. "Wheel the unit out."

"Decision noted," said Matthew. "Execution proceeds."

There was a short hissing noise as air was readmitted to the matter receiver. Matthew released the vacuum seal. The door of the matter receiver swung open.

Mark pulled out a titanium cylinder. It moved easily on its built-in rollers. Identification had been stencilled on the cylinder.

In large letters there was the word: Engineer. Underneath that there was small lettering: Jean Mitterand, age twenty-seven, I.Q. 149, road-builder, French citizen.

"Welcome to Tantalus, Monsieur Mitterand," said Conrad to the cylinder. "You will have many roads to construct." He turned to Mark. "Wheel him to the storage chamber."

"Decision noted. Execution proceeds."

Matthew said: "Permission requested to recommence reception cycle."

"Permission granted."

"Decision noted. Execution proceeds."

The next one came out of the matter receiver a few minutes later. The cylinder was stencilled: Doctor. Tore Rudefors, age thirty-three, I.Q. 157, specialist gynecology, Swedish citizen.

"Welcome, Tore Rudefors. May you deliver many babies on Tantalus," said Conrad. "Wheel him away."

And so it went on.

Conrad stayed to watch the arrival of the next ten. Kwango and Zonis left at number five. Presumably, they had something better to do than watch titanium cylinders being wheeled out of the matter receiver and placed in storage.

Lieutenant Smith stayed.

She moved close to Conrad. She held his hand. He didn't seem to notice.

Unit eleven—Teacher: Natalie Remarque, I.Q. 131, Australian citizen—was wheeled away.

"James! It's all happening and it's all O.K."

"Yes, love, it's all happening and it's all O.K. Indira, can you bring ten out tomorrow? Matthew can help you with resuscitation procedure. Dammit, we can all help."

"*Déja vu,*" said Indira. "It was like this on Kratos. You remember?"

"Yes, I remember."

"Then remember Applecross also. It is important."

"We'll get there again," said Conrad. "I promise."

Indira smiled. "I'll hold you to that."

Conrad scratched his silver eye-patch nervously. "Can you bring ten out tomorrow?"

"James Conrad, you are a bastard and I love you."

"Yes, but—"

Indira flung her arms round him and there were no more buts.

MEMORANDUM

To: Secretary General, United Nations.
From: Director, Extra-Solar Planets Evaluating and Normalising Department. Most Secret. For your eyes only.
Subject: The proving of Tantalus, 7th planet Alpha Leonis (Regulus), distance 56 light years.
9th January 2076 S.E.T.
Para 1. With the successful proving of Tantalus and the transmission of the first thousand colonists, Third World opposition to the ExPEND programme is rapidly fading. This is partly due to the fact that a high proportion of Third World candidates have been accepted for current and future colonisation projects. Bearing this new situation in mind, I earnestly recommend that no action be taken in the case of Lisa Uhlmann. Commander Conrad requests that she should be charged with mutiny, destruction of U.N. property and attempted murder. Technically, he is within his rights in requiring trial by court-martial. However, the evidence that the defense might produce in such a trial could be embarrassing not only to certain eminent Third World statesmen (who now give tacit approval to our programme) but to ExPEND itself. When Commander Conrad is appraised of the current political situation, I do not think he will press his legitimate demand for a trial. If he should do so, however, I have

sworn statements from three distinguished psychiatrists of international repute that Uhlmann has experienced extreme trauma and is unfit to plead.

Para 2. The proved existence on Tantalus of a now defunct colony of technologically advanced creatures has created a delicate problem. The international scientific community is in furore, and I have been deluged with applications from archaeologists, anthropologists and scientists of almost every class for permission to investigate and analyse the remains of the rings of Tantalus. It appears to me that we shall have to mount an expedition quite separate from the colonisation programme. May I have your advice? If such an expedition were mounted, substantial additional funds would be needed to finance it. As you are aware, the ExPEND budget is allocated solely for the proving and colonisation of extra-solar planets.

Para 3. The choice of the name Kheladelphia for the first city on Tantalus has been of immense value in cooling the traditional Arab-Israeli hostility. Naturally, the account of Ahmed Khelad's assault upon Ruth Zonis remains classified information. Zonis is an intelligent woman. She appreciates what would happen if the truth were known. I recomment that she be awarded the U.N. Gold Medallion for services rendered on Tantalus.

File Closed